I0664846

Loving Topaz

Copyright 2011 by James Colwell

Cover design by James Colwell

All rights reserved. No part of this book may be
reproduced, stored, or transmitted in any form or by
any means, graphic, electronic, mechanical, including
photocopying, recording, taping, or by any information
storage retrieval system, without the permission in
writing from the author.

Printed in the United States of America.

For licensing/copyright information, additional copies
or for use in specialized settings contact:

James Colwell

412-322-6464

www.JCNovels.com
Email: whenjcspeaks@msn.com

Loving Topaz

Table of Contents

<u>Meet the Bailleaus</u>

My name is Eugene, Eugene Bailleau. I'm 16 years old and a junior at Solitz High School. Now, my close friends actually call me Topaz, and I'll explain why in a moment. I am the youngest of three, I have a 19 year old sister named TriAnn and an 18 year old brother named Edward. My mom is a pretty cool chic, she's 32 and her name is Theresa. My mom is kind of fly, she's built really cute, and a lot of folks think she's our sister. My sister really hates that; almost as much as she hates me, if that's even possible. TriAnn is interesting, she has her own place, so I don't see her much, we have never really gotten along. She thinks I'm weird and an embarrassment to her, so she has always been kind of mean to me. So, recently I stopped taking TriAnn's crap and started speaking up for myself, so we really just don't talk. My mom gets mad at us for this, but what can I do, I'm gay and it is what it is. I'm sorry ole girl don't like it. She has ripped me to shreds about this for as long as I can remember. She used to call me faggot and sissy, when I didn't even know what that was. I have learned not to care what she thinks. A lot of times I really think she is a little jealous. My sis is a bit self-centered, her and my mom can't seem to get along either. It's like she thinks she is always right; no matter what my mom says about anything, it's a guarantee that TriAnn will always disagree. My mom says it's because they kinda grew up together. You see, mom's only 13 years older than TriAnn. But whatever, I just think that TriAnn is disrespectful and evil. And speaking of evil, is my total opposite sibling, Edward. We are really two different sides of the street. Where I am smaller and more petite, he is muscular and stands about 6 foot, 1 inch tall. I am fun and tend to smile a lot; Ed doesn't say much and is very standoffish. Really, thugged out if you will. Ed sells drugs and lives a dangerous type of life, he has been out of the house since he was 15. Mom told him to go and live with his dad, since he acts like that group of vultures. Yes, the three of us have different fathers. Like I said my mom is young and fly, some of her choices haven't been the best, but she has always done right by me and my siblings. When she put Edward out of the house, she cried for days. I could hear her sobbing through the walls whenever she would be alone in her room. She told him that no child of hers was gonna jeopardize the life or the lifestyle that she has worked so hard to create for us here. Ed is hard-headed though, he likes the fast money and stuff that his lifestyle brings, and the other side of his family is really into that life. His own dad is the one the turned him onto the life. My mom has an idea that this is how it all got started, but she doesn't have any proof of it, but either way, she really hates Ed's pops, they really don't talk at all.

    That is really kind of the way that mom is; when she is done with you, she is done, there's no going back. The only person I've ever known her to forgive for hurting her is TriAnn. Mom bends over backwards to get along with her and to keep a somewhat healthy relationship with my evil-ass sister. It's really sad, and it makes me kind of mad, because TriAnn uses mom up when she needs something and then at other times she acts like mom is her worst enemy.

Oh wow, how could I forget, there is one more person that my mom seems to always give second chances to, Whalid!

Whalid Jesper is my mom's 27 year old boyfriend. They've been kickin' it for about a year and a half now. My brother Ed doesn't like Whalid being around at all, he always says, "That nigga ain't all that he say he is!" Ed doesn't want him with mom at all. TriAnn says that mom needs to grow up and find a man her own age. Again, I swear that girl is just jealous, she doesn't have a man of her own, her age or otherwise. I don't have any problems with Whalid, I think he is really cool, he lives in the house with me and mom and he's always really nice to me. Whalid's been living in the house with us for the last nine months or so, and he has never made any type of gay slurs or said any rude comments about my walk or clothing choices. He always says stuff like, "You gotta be you Baby Boy!" And he always tells me how important it is for me to comfortable with myself.

The crazy thing is, Whalid is the one that named me Topaz. I liked it and it just stuck. My mom doesn't know that, he said we'll keep it between us, so as not to piss mom off. She says she's cool about my sexuality, but sometimes I'm not so sure. Anyway, Whalid said, "All the girls in your family have names that begin with a T, and you should too." He continued on explaining to me that he thinks that topaz is the most beautiful and precious thing that he has ever seen and he feels the name fits. So, that's where I got the nickname from, yet I've never told anyone. Whenever mom's in the house Whalid calls me Baby Boy, but whenever no one else is around he calls me Topaz or T for short.

TriAnn Sets It Off

"Gene…Gene…Gene…Eugene Bailleau!" I heard my mom calling and getting louder and louder. I slowly roll over and see my digital clock glaring 7:32am. Gosh, is she serious? Just then my door begins to open slowly and I start to see a head of dreads peaking through the opening and I hear, "Baby Boy…" I tried to act like I didn't hear him. A few seconds passed and he said, "Topaz, don't play, I know you hear me, get up, your mom's calling you." I raised my head up a little and said, "Whalid, it's too early." He chuckled and said, "I know, but you know how she is.

Get yo lil ass up before she bring her loud ass up here. Let's go T, we got a lot of work to do before these folks start to showin' up." With of wink of his eye, the dreads started to disappear from my view and the door began to close slowly. I laid there for about another five minutes before I arose. I was excited thinking, this is the first time I will have friends of mine come over for a family cookout. It put a smile on my face just thinking about it. For the first time, I can spend my time in conversations and interactions that truly involve me. This is gonna be fun.

Once I was fully dressed I was ready to roll. I stood in front of my full-length mirror that hangs on the back of my bedroom door and took in my outfit, I was pleased with it. I was wearing a shirt that my friend Mike had made; he is an aspiring designer. The mesh, sleeveless tank was very fitted and cut off just above my navel and the fabric looked like an American flag. It was perfect, it showed off my new belly-button piercing which was adorned with a miniature flag. I had on a dark blue pair of True Religion jeans that were loose at my waist and kind of laid right at my hipline. And of course, I had a new pair of red, white and blue Nikes. I looked hott. As I backed up from the mirror, pleased with my vision, I said to myself, "Happy 4th of July."

As I declined the stairs I could hear my mom in the kitchen talking to Whalid, "Where is that boy? He better get his ass on down here, I need him to mix this potato salad and season this chicken for the grill." Whalid snickered and replied, "C'mon Bae, you know damn well Baby Boy ain't fuckin' wit that raw chicken and shit when he gets his stuff all hooked up!" Mom sneered, "Huh, his pretty ass better go change then, cause that ass is cookin' this morning!" At that moment I hit the bend and stuck my head in the kitchen. Mom threw me a quick little smug look, and as I came into full view she froze for a moment and said, "Boy, what da hell is that?" I said, "What?" "That shit on your stomach, I know it better not be real," she blurted as she flopped into one of the kitchen chairs. "It is Ma, what's wrong with that?" I paused and looked in her eyes, they were blank and just a little confused. The awkward silence was broken by the deep chuckle coming from the now visibly entertained, Whalid. "What's up Threa - let that boy do his thing, he ain't hurtin' nobody." My mom snapped at him, "It just ain't necessary…that's all!" "What ain't necessary Bae? What is he doin? Y'all be trippin' man, y'all need to leave that boy alone!" Now standing in front of my mom and visibly irritated was Whalid's toned, 6 foot 3 inch Adonis-like body. I just watched as my mom's demeanor faded like a patch of fog, she purred, "You're right Boo, I'm trippin'. Gene go on and change them clothes so you can help me cook." Whalid looked over at me and winked, and though I felt a bit attacked by my mom, knowing Whalid had my back made the sting of it all fade quickly. As I cut out of the kithen and went back around the bend to go back upstairs, I seen my mom grab the waistband on Whalid's denim shorts, which made the top button pop open, which loosened them enough that they came down a bit exposing his pubic region, he grabbed the waistband and said, "Chill, stop playin' Threa." Mom chuckled and cooed. I thought to myself, "Yuck! And, does that boy ever wear underwear? That's like his trademark. Just running around going commando. He mostly wears sweats or basketball shorts which basically exposes all his business, and he's got plenty of business to be seen. I guess that's where all my mom's cooing and purring stems from; just a mess.

We finally finished preparing all the food around 1:30pm and I was jumping back out of the shower and getting redressed when I heard my sister's voice echoing through the house, "Hey y'all, Happy 4th! I'm ready to get it in, and I'm so hungry, what we havin'?" Then I heard my mom say, "Hey, how you girls doin' today, thanks for comin' over!" TriAnn brought her two good friends Angie and Nati with her. They are cool girls, I have never had any issues with them, though they do tend to get really tickled when TriAnn acts out viciously. A few moments later I heard TriAnn say, "Where's my bro? I ain't seen that nigga in a minute." As I reached the end of the hallway and began down the staircase I heard mom say, "Getting dressed, you know how…" She was abruptly interrupted when TriAnn said, "Ma please, I said my bro, not the family weirdo! You know damn well I ain't lookin' for him, I'm talkin' bout Ed!" Mom replied firmly, "TriAnn, don't start that today." By this time I had

reached the bottom of the stairs and Angie and Nati
said, "Hey Gene!" I just waived and kept it moving
toward the front door, the bell was ringing, I was
hoping it was my guests, but it wasn't. It was
Whalid's parents, Mr. and Mrs. Jesper. They are a
very nice couple; they are both in their fifties and
Whalid is their only child. He always tells me he is
spoiled, sometimes when him and mom get to going at
she calls him a Mama's boy, he hates it. I invited
them in and told them that I would go and tell Whalid
that they had arrived; they came in and headed for the
kitchen area where everyone was beginning to gather.
I started up the stairs and I could hear that the
shower in my mom's room was not on so I tapped on the
bedroom door and then opened it. As I opened the door
I got stopped in my tracks, standing there looking
like a perfectly chiseled naked statue was Whalid
putting on lotion. I was stuck right where I stood,
and I nervously said, "Whalid, I'm sorry, I thought
you were dressed, I didn't hear the shower…but anyway
your mom and dad are here." Without flinching or
trying to hide his nakedness he chuckled and said,
"OK, and don't worry about it, you got the same thing

I do, no harm done." As I fought to make my feet go in a turning motion to get me out of there, I told myself, "Yeah, we got the same thing, but surely I was not given as much as you, damn!"

As I reached the bottom of the staircase the bell rang again, when I got to the door I was so happy, this time it was my guests. Standing there on my porch was Mike, Quan and Jamal. "C'mon in y'all!" Mike entered the door first and whispered in my ear, "Hey Topaz, sexy ass." Quan came right behind him, and as I was ready to shut the door I noticed Jamal was still standing on the porch, I said, "Wassup, Jay-Jay?" He replied, "Chile, is yo sister up in there?" I said, "Yes, she's here and she done already said some ole slick shit outta her mouth about me. But don't worry she don't know you, she won't bother you!" You see, Jamal is like my therapist when it comes to dealing with the things that I go through with TriAnn, though he has never met her, he knows how she gets down. I tell him a lot, that he is more of a sister to me than she is. Quan came back to the door and grabbed Jamal's hand and said, "C'mon baby, you worry too much."

Quan is a cool ass dude, he and Jamal(Jay-Jay as we call him) have been dating since we were in ninth grade. Where Jay-Jay is a lot like me, flamboyant and quite noticeably gay. If Quan didn't tell you, you wouldn't know. The same kind of goes for Mike; other than his love for fashion, there is nothing feminine about him at all, the girls at the school are always on him. He has even dated a few of them, but nothing serious has come out of any of that business. He says he is waiting on me so that he can get settled down. Whatever; I like Mike and I find him to be attractive, but I don't know if I like him like that. Though he is so nice to me and always makes me clothes and stuff, buys me little gifts, I mean he is really a sweet person. He understands that I am not ready to be sexually active and he doesn't even push that, he says he is cool with it, and whenever I'm ready, he is dying to be my first. I know that he is sincere; I did let him kiss me once last summer. It was ok, until he proceeded to try to touch me below the belt. I broke from his embrace and ran all the way home, it kind of scared me; it was too much, way too fast. He apologized constantly for four months; I kept telling him everything was cool, but he just kept apologizing.

I led my friends to the now quite full kitchen; all eyes were on us, as I said, "Hey everyone, I'd like to introduce you all to my best friends in the world, this is Quan, Mike and Jay-Jay. It's their first time with us, let's make them feel welcome." Not two seconds later I hear a little rumbling and laughter coming from the corner where TriAnn and her two friends were sitting, I shot her a dirty look, and she stands up walks over toward the fridge and says aloud, "Oh great, more fruit loops!" My mom stood up and said, "Welcome to our home guys, help yourself to whatever you'd like, we have plenty. We are glad to finally meet y'all, Gene talks about y'all all the time." At that time Whalid stood up next to my mom and said, "Yeah, fellas if y'all need anything, let one of us know, and thanks for coming over to spend time with Baby Boy." I was pretty impressed at how my family was trying to clean up TriAnn's rude comment. Whalid's dad, Mr. Jester said, "Yeah, Happy 4th of July, let's eat everybody!" TriAnn left the room like a spoiled child, and her friends followed behind her.

We all got our plates together and something to drink and walked out of the sliding glass doors in our kitchen onto the deck where several other family members were gathering. My uncle Joe hollered out, "Wassup Lil' Gene, come give your unc' some love!" I walked over and gave him a hug. Uncle Joe is my moms' older brother, he is 35 and still lives with my grandma. He has a decent job working for the city, but never got his own place, he will move out and go live with different women from time to time but always ends up back with my grandma. When my grandfather was still living, he couldn't stand it, he always said, "Joseph, you need to get yourself an address, what kind of grown-ass man ain't got no address!" Boy would they go at it about that comment, it still makes me laugh to this day. Uncle Joe said, "Boy let me see what this outfit is doin' that you're wearin'. My uncle gave me one good long look and said, "I like dat shit for you, dat shit's nice neph'! I don't know where you find dat kinda shit; it don't be in the store when I'm in there." I laughed and told my uncle about Mike making my shirt. He said, "Hell yeah, dats wassup, y'all come on over and meet Uncle Joe, if

y'all friends of my nephew, then y'all my nephews too.
Y'all lil niggas come gimme some love!" I introduced
them to my uncle one at a time, he gave Quan and Mike
a pound and when he got to Jay-Jay, Jay-Jay extended
his hand to get a pound, when my uncle held his head
back and bust out laughing. A look of confusion fell
over Jay-Jay's face and all at once my uncle pulled
Jay-Jay to him and embraced him and said, "Don't ever
try to be something you're not wit' Uncle Joe; you
hear me. I'm cool wit' everything bout me, I gets
more pussy than I can use. I love my nephew, and I
don't give a fuck what nobody say, dats my Lil' Gene,
I love 'em like a son. I always said my sis had him
for me. I ain't got no kids, I can't have none…" I
interrupted, "Uncle Joe, you ain't got to…" "Hush up
neph', it's cool, I want your friends to know where
I'm comin' from. C'mon over here lil niggas, y'all
sit down wit your Uncle Joe, I'ma spit some shit at
y'all!" We all sat down, there were about four or
five of my other older cousins outside sitting on the
benches and tables on the deck, and Uncle Joe had the
floor, as he began to speak again. "Back some years
ago, I was wit' the woman I loved, we was perfect

together man, I believe she was the only woman I have really been in love wit'. And I done had plenty of women, I ain't goin' lie. Her name was Theresa, just like my baby sis, spelled the same and everything. I had asked her to marry me and we found out about a month later she was knocked up; man I was happy. Then my world got all fucked up. We was comin' home from a party on New Years Eve, the snow was bad as shit man, I was being real careful you know cause I had my wifey and she was carryin' my lil' shawty. All the traffic had slowed down 'cause there was an accident up ahead; we eventually came to a stand still. We were there about ten minutes or so when out of nowhere I heard some sliding and skidding and shit and when I looked in the mirror I could see the car coming and wasn't shit I could do. They hit us in the back, which pushed us into the car in front of us, it happened so fuckin' quick. I kept calling Theresa's name, but she ain't say shit. She was unconscious which didn't really make me worry right away; the ambulance and all that got there kind of quick. Fuck, I was up and at 'em, nothing was wrong 'wit me, I just felt like I got shook around real bad, like a bad-ass kid wit' a big ass head; know what I mean. Then I seen my Boo, she was all bloody and shit. Her seat belt had broken and the none of the air bags came out, which we found out later was due to a defect wit' my ride. The impact had slammed her head into the windshield and her belly into the dashboard. Her and the baby were pronounced dead on the scene, they told me that she didn't suffer cause she was gone on the impact. That didn't make me feel no better; I was fucked up! I was walking around in a daze for about two days, I was over at my mom and dad's, because I couldn't stand going back to the apartment that we lived in. I was coming down the steps on the third day and outta nowhere it felt like somebody grabbed my balls and locked them in a vice grip; I passed the fuck out. When I woke up, I was at the Emergency Room; they told me I had been walking around in shock, and what they found out, is that when the steering wheel hit my stomach it fucked my shit up. I was bleeding on the inside, and long story short, I have a fucked up sperm count now and I can't produce babies. It was fucked up, I got some good money out of all of it, but I would give it all back in a second for me to have my family back. And the really fucked up thing is, Theresa's family still don't wanna have shit to do wit' me; they blamed me for the death even with all of the evidence. But about two months later I found out my sister's dude was spankin' dat ass, and I had to come over and spank his. Dude was a trip, but after woopin' on dat ass and eventually moving in with my sis and her oldest two kids, we found out that my sis was pregnant and all that fightin' and shit was fuckin' wit the baby. Her pregnancy was shitty; it was hell man. So I stayed over here wit' them; she ended up on bed rest. But 'bout five and half months later came the prettiest baby I ever seen man!" I looked up at my uncle he had a tear in his eye. He got up walked over to me and put his hands on my shoulders and said, "That was my nephew, I knew I was goin' take care of him for the rest of my life man. My sis almost lost him a couple of times during her pregnancy, I kept telling her, don't worry, that is my baby and God wouldn't take two of 'em from me. And when Lil' Gene came, man it was the first day of the rest of my life, I always told your mom, he ain't gotta worry 'bout nothin'. That's my baby." I was absolutely in tears by this time; I knew some of the story but I had never heard the whole ordeal. Everybody was kind of quiet as well. With tears streaming down his face, Jay-Jay looked at me and said, "You are blessed to have somebody love you like that." My uncle walked over to Jay-Jay and grabbed his arm and said, "Wassup; your family don't accept you and shit?" Jay-Jay looked up and said, "No, not really." My uncle grabbed him in a tight hug and said, "Fuck that, you got a family here, you hear me! Now you gotchu an Uncle named Joe, and if a muthafucka get wrong tell 'em Joe Bailleau will fuck some shit up! I'm serious Lil' Jay, you're our family now, fuck the dumb shit!" He kissed Jay-Jay on the forehead as he released him from his embrace. My other cousins that were sitting in the area nodded in agreement and a couple of them said, "Yeah, you're part of our family now!"

Just as the mood began to become a little lighter and we were really enjoying ourselves on the deck, TriAnn and her two friends came out of the sliding door. Nati said, "Hey Gene, I wanted to tell you, I love your outfit, you look real cute, and what's your other friend's name that has the belly shirt on?" I said, "Yeah, Mike made both of our shirts, and his name is…" My Uncle chimed in, "You talkin' 'bout this pretty lil muthafucka here?" As he pulled Jay-Jay over by his arm, "This is my new nephew, Lil' Jay!" Nati said, "I know that's right Mr. Joe; I do like what y'all wearing, y'all look hott!"

Then out of nowhere, I heard, "Them faggots do not look hott, that bullshit ain't cute and that Bitch is no relation to us. It's bad enough, we got the one that we can't get rid of." Everyone just got quiet and looked. I said, "TriAnn, why don't you go somewhere and sit down, ain't nobody bothering you, you've been at it all day and nobody is interested; we're trying to have a good time." She started walking toward me yelling, "You damn right ain't nobody goin' bother me, I'll turn this muthafucka out. Fuck you and your weird ass friends, especially you and that other funny dressing Bitch; running around in them half shirts, y'all ain't no girls. Niggas in the streets are laughin' at your asses; don't nobody like that bullshit." I looked in Jay-Jay's face, I could see the tears welling up in his eyes. I know that's when he's gettings to that point when he is about to

go off. I walked over and grabbed his hand and said,
"I'm so sorry, please ignore her ignorant ass." A few
seconds later she had turned her rant onto Mike and
Quan, she stood in front of them and said, "Why y'all
wanna be some fags? Y'all look normal, but y'all some
bitch-ass niggas too, that shit is disgusting!" My
Uncle Joe yelled out, "Shut the fuck up and go on
somewhere TriAnn, that shit don't make no sense. Go
the fuck on girl!" TriAnn tried to bass up at my
uncle, "I ain't gotta go nowhere! This is my mother's
house, you don't like what I got to say, you can leave
and take all them Sweet Tarts with you; fuckin'
bitches!" My mom had reached the deck by then and
figured out what was going on. My uncle said,
"Theresa, that girl is trippin', and I'm not having
her talk to me like that!" My mom replied, "I know
Joe, I'm gonna talk to her." My uncle slammed his
hand on the table he was sitting at, "Talk, ain't
nothing left to say, she needs her ass wooped, she on
some ole bullshit! I love you sis, but I'm out!" My
uncle proceeded to leave out of our yard through the
back gate, he was so mad that he wouldn't even walk
through the house to get to his car, which was parked

in the front of the house. As he reached the end of

the yard, he hollered, "I love y'all, all my nephews,

new and old; you hear me. Uncle Joe loves y'all!"

All the cousins that were sitting out there with us

left as well. I took my guests and had them follow me

in the house, as I reached the kitchen, I could see

Whalid and his parents sitting there, I immediately

started to apologize to them for all of the commotion.

Whalid said, "Baby Boy don't do that, we heard the

whole thing, y'all ain't done nothing to apologize

for!" I could tell right away he was pissed off with

the situation. Mrs. Jesper said, "Don't worry about

it Sweet Baby, we've heard it all before. Me and Wade

are old; you name it we've seen it and heard it. Why

don't you take your guests out onto the front porch

and try to enjoy the rest of this day. You children

are gracious; you took quite a few hard verbal blows

and handled yourselves like true gentlemen, and that

is to be celebrated!" Mr. Jesper nodded his head in

agreement.

Just as we were leaving the kitchen, the back

door flew open and in came TriAnn like a bolt of

lightning, she was screaming something about hating me

and being tired of being embarrassed when I'm around,
I couldn't hear it all because by the time I was
trying to zero in on what she was saying my face had
hit the wall. She had a death grip on the back of my
shirt and she was punching me repeatedly, I eventually
lost my balance and was on the ground face down.
TriAnn weighs over two hundred pounds and she is
solid, I couldn't move. She continued to punch me in
my back and in the back of my head. Everything was
moving so quickly that some of it is still a blur.
Whalid leaped up and grabbed TriAnn off of me, I
remember him yelling, "Are you crazy!!!!!" As he was
getting her off me, she was pulling my shirt, which
was now torn quite a bit and the mesh was choking me
pretty badly. In the midst of it I did catch a
glimpse of Mike being dragged down the hallway to the
front door by Quan and Jay-Jay; I am glad, I wouldn't
have wanted him involved any further in this fiasco.
By the time I was free, I was lying on the kitchen
floor and my mom was screaming at Whalid not to hit
TriAnn. Whalid was screaming back, "I would never do
that, I would never hit a woman. All I was doing is
stopping her from killing your son!" Mr. and Mrs.

Jesper had helped me up off of the floor by this time and we were standing near the entrance to the hallway. Whalid was still holding TriAnn, as she was trying to break free to attack me again, he told her to calm down or he wasn't going to let her go. As I stood there looking like I had been in a train wreck, I could not believe what I was hearing. At this point my mom was going on a rant and saying, "The two of you have ruined this holiday and it doesn't make any sense!" It was classic, TriAnn acts a fool, but total blame is never given to her for her antics. Well, I'd had enough, this time she had taken it too far.

I said to my mom, "Are you serious? Are you going to sit there and act like you didn't watch this whole ridiculous episode unfold. She started being mean and talking crap about me the moment she came into the house today. Yeah, I heard the cow talking mess before I came down the steps earlier, I'm sick of this crap, you…" I was abruptly interrupted by my mom, "I what boy, and I'll not have you talk shit to me, cause I'll set this muthafucka off!" I couldn't believe my ears, I just walked down the hall and out of the front door onto the porch, all of my guests

were gone. I was absolutely embarrassed and
disgusted. After about twenty minutes, Mr. and Mrs.
Jesper came out and Mrs. Jesper said, "Sweet Baby,
you're coming home with us tonight, I smoothed it over
with your mama and we think it's best that you sleep
over with us and everybody will have time to cool off.
We love this family and want the best for all of you.
Just come on, you don't need anything, you can use any
of the stuff that is in Whalid's old room." I said,
"Thank you so much." I followed them down the front
steps and into their car. I continued crying the
whole twenty minute drive over to the Jesper's home.

Overnight At The Jesper's

After reaching the Jesper's home it was strange to me, but I immediately started to feel at ease. They have a beautiful home, I've been there a few times before but never without Whalid, and I had never gono upstairs. Mrs Jesper immediately took me up to Whalid's old room, she told me to make myself at home, take a bath and help myself to some of Whalid's clothes. She suggested that I get some rest, by this time it was already about 11 pm. Whalid's room was almost exactly like my room at home but it was huge, my bedroom has a bathroom in it as well, but my gosh,

Whalid's bathroom was almost as big as my room itself.

I sat on the chair at his desk for awhile looking in

the mirror, I had scratches on my cheeks and my neck.

My neck was also a little swollen. I was really sore

all over, I decided to get up and go to take a bath,

just then I realized that I had forgotten my cell

phone at home in the kitchen on the counter, I wanted

to make sure my friends were ok, and to let them know

I was alright; that would have to wait.

I stayed in the tub soaking for quite awhile, all

the bubbles had gone away and my water was becoming

luke warm, I figured it was time to get out. I found

a pair of sweatpants in one of Whalid's drawers, of

course they were way to big, I pulled the drawstring

as tight as I could. Upon hitting that king size bed

I was out like a light, I awoke to a feeling that

someone was touching my face, and then my head. I

opened my eyes and was a little startled because there

he was; Whalid was sitting on the edge of the bed

rubbing the top of my head. He said, "I didn't mean

to wake you up, I just wanted to make sure you were

alright. I was back at the house and I couldn't

sleep, thinkin' 'bout how all that shit jumped off. Me and your mom have been arguing up a storm, she doesn't want to admit that she was wrong, and your sis; man someone's got to sit and talk to her; she is like a crazy person, but for no reason." I sat up and noticed the clock said it was 2:35am, and like Whalid said he was in bed before he came over, he was wearing pajama pants and a tank top. I stood up and said, "Let me go to the bathroom." When I came back I was struggling again with that doggone drawstring, the pants were still almost falling off of me. Whalid began to laugh at me, he said, "You are so damn little T, and yeah earlier, wassup with you not wearin' underwear, what was you doin? I noticed it and said to myself that I was goin ask you. That Mike dude noticed too, he was all in your face, wassup wit' him and you." I sat back on the bed and said, "He's cool and he does like me like that, but I'm not really sure how I feel about him. I did let him kiss me once last summer but that's it." Whalid pushed his dreads back out of his face and said, "That better be all that went on! What you even know bout that lil nigga? Anyway, enough about that, how you feeling, you got some scratches and shit." I dropped my head down and said, "I know, I don't even want anybody seeing me like this. I could kill TriAnn! And mom… I am so mad at them I could just…" Whalid stopped me and grabbed my head and said, "Don't worry T, nobody is gonna do that to you again, and you don't have to worry about your looks, you are the prettiest nigga I know, you're aight Baby Boy – Beautiful, just like topaz." After that, a silence was in the room, he still had my head in his hands and was just looking at me. I stared back at him, it was weird, he had lived with us for over nine months and I never looked at him like I had been lately. Before I knew anything our lips were touching and though it was weird, I like it and it felt safe. He pulled his head away and said, "This is wrong T, but I can't help myself, tell me if you want me to stop. I pray that you don't, but I will if you want me to." I really didn't want him to stop, it was like my soul was crying out to his and my whole body was heating up from the inside. I tried to start more conversation to deter the physical tension, I said, "And for the record man, I had on underwear earlier, it was just a fake out, I pulled them down low so they wouldn't show. He swiftly slid his hand down the waistband of my sweats and slowly around and softly cupped my behind and said, "But you don't have any on now, though!" I could hear and feel my breath escaping my body through my mouth in a frantic sigh. I knew there was no going back, he kissed me again, and this time pushed his tongue into my mouth, it was like someone lit firecrackers inside of me, I was on fire and I was going to take the leap and let Whalid put it out!

He stood up and walked over to turn out the light and lock the door, I gave him a good look and everything he had was standing very attentively; I got a little nervous. That didn't last long, by the time he made it back over to the bed he had stripped down to nothing, he said, "I know this is your first time so just follow my lead, OK." I nodded and went with the flow, within seconds I was naked, once he embraced me all the nervousness had dissipated. It was the most extraordinary experience I have ever had, he literally talked me through every aspect of what went on, from showing me the best way to kiss him to putting the condom on him. I felt as though we were one, there is not one place on my body for which he did not put his mouth or his hands, and I loved every minute of it. And when it ended it got even better, we slept with me totally embraced in his muscular frame, I have never felt so wanted or so safe.

I awoke and looked over at the clock, it was 9:43am. I was still fully engulfed in Whalid's grasp, I went to get loose and I heard him say, "Did I tell you to go anywhere? What's your rush, is something wrong, did I hurt you?" I said, "No, not at all, but don't you have to go to work, and what about your parents?" He paused and said, "I'm off today and my parents are gone, my mom and I talked when I came in last night, she knew I was here so she didn't bother to wake us. Now I have a question for you Topaz." He kissed me softly on the back of my neck and said, "Can I have some more of you?" I felt like I was going to melt, and in an instant the kiss on the neck turned into him running his tongue straight down the crease in my back stopping at the small of my back. I didn't know what to do with myself, I started trying to move away from him, his touch was driving me crazy. He rolled over and pinned me down and said, "Don't go nowhere T, I'm gettin' ready to show you something totally different, it may make you scream and there's nobody's here so if you want, you can go ahead, OK. Just let me have you, alright T?" I got nervous all over again, but I trusted him so I nodded in agreement. He leaned up off me and said, "Can you show me how flexible you are." I gave him a puzzled look; he then took my leg and began to stretch it upward toward my head. His face lit up in excitement, then he said, "Shit yeah, you got dat good-good, I'm 'bout to give you all I got, are you ready?" I didn't know what the heck was getting ready to go on, but I just shook my head yes.

We got started and it was completely different than what we did the night before, where it was slow and sensual, this was more exciting and acrobatic. But, equally as enjoyable, and as he said there were points that I just yelled out his name, I couldn't help it. And I guess he couldn't either, because I heard my name being used quite a few times. He put me on the desk, on the dresser, on the floor, against the wall and at a few points he just literally carried me around and had his way with me as I was airborne.

After about an hour and a half, I was exhausted. We went back to sleep for a few hours, about 3pm we were showered and dressed and heading home. As I sat in the passenger seat of Whalid's SUV, I couldn't stop staring at the porch of the Jesper home, for I knew that 16 year old, Eugene Bailleau had been left there and Topaz had truly risen like a phoenix and there was no going back, I knew that I had been forever changed that day.

Change Is Scary

The ride back to our house was interesting to say the least. At certain times we just found ourselves looking at each other. I was thinking about how I had not really paid much attention to Whalid, and now I couldn't take my eyes off of him. Everything about him now seems to make a slight sensation on the inside of me. Even the bass in his voice made my stomach quiver. He was just staring at me while we were at a red light and he said, "Goddamn you are so fuckin' beautiful T. I don't know what we are going to do, this shit's crazy. You know I love you right? But now I…I don't know…damn!" I turned my head and looked out of the window and I said, "Whalid, I'm not a child, I know we are in a weird place. It should've never happened, but I ain't trippin' off of it, you are my mom's boyfriend and that's not gonna change, it's on me to deal with now. I'm not gonna say anything, it's our secret, but I don't regret it – It is what it is!" Whalid's eyebrows kind of raised up as he said, "What the fuck you mean, it is what it is T? I don't want you thinkin' I just dicked you down and oh well. That ain't what we did. You're more to me than that…" I turned my body toward him and said, "Really, I guess I am, technically you're my stepdad, isn't that cute! I'm not getting caught up in this, and you know it's over, just like I know it. It really never got started, don't play with me, please don't do that." I could tell Whalid was getting a little irritated with me, which never lasts long, but today he wasn't backing away from his discontentment with me. He pulled the car over as we approached the parking lot of my school, which was about another ten minutes from my house. He turned the car off, and turned his body toward me. I could see he was getting angry, which didn't bother me, I knew he wouldn't hit me or anything so I didn't even flinch. He said, "This ain't you T, you don't just throw yourself away and then act like, what the fuck! I will not even let you be like that, you're better than that Baby. I took your virginity and you're sitting here acting like it wasn't shit!" I was starting to get mad now because he just wouldn't let it go. I said, "What makes you think I was a virgin, I don't tell you everything about me. You ain't got me all pegged…" Whalid grabbed my arm tightly and pulled me in to him and said, "You tryin' to fuck wit' me Topaz and I'm gettin' pissed off! And don't try to tell me no shit 'bout you not being a virgin, you ain't gotta tell me that nobody has had dat ass, I been watching it for almost two years now. And besides when I ran up in it, I could tell that I was the one and only one that has been there. So don't say no shit like dat to me no more, you hear me!" At that moment a single tear ran down my cheek. I felt so stupid, I felt like I had been stalked and captured. Had he been really watching me around the house like he said and just made his move on me when he got the chance? I was too upset to even voice my concerns. About two minutes later the rest of the tears came, I was breaking down pretty badly when Whalid lifted my head and said, "Don't do that, stop, don't do that T. I can't take it, I can't stand to see you cry. Please quit it, I'm sorry. It's just I been on you forever, and it's something that I'm really ashamed of and shit. You was like 12 the first time I seen you around the neighborhood and I was like damn, I didn't oven know why I was being attracted to you. The weird thing is, it wasn't anything sexual, I just thought you were different and you wasn't scared of it. You were prettier than most little girls your age and besides I ain't never wanted to be wit' no dude. A little bit after that is when I met Threa, and I always thought she looked like somebody I knew, but couldn't figure out who. By the time I found out you were her son, you were like 13 and you know the rest. I really do like your mom and our relationship; but more than that, I love being close, to be able to protect you, and then the older you got the more attractive you became, it's weird…" I interrupted him, "So now I'm weird, is this supposed to make me feel better?" Whalid put his hand over my mouth softly and said, "Please Boo-Bear, let me explain myself." I pulled his hand away from my mouth and said, "Boo-Bear?" Whalid rolled his eyes up in his head and said, "T seriously, stop it. Like I was saying, it's kind of weird how after awhile I stopped even looking at you as a boy. I mean, you ain't got no hair nowhere on your body, your face and skin is so damn soft and your ass is…my God." He reached down in his crotch and rubbed his business and said, "I just sat back a watched as you became the beautiful piece of work that you are. I mean, I got so jealous when you told me that lil' clothes making dude had kissed you, I wanted to fuck him up, but they would throw my ass in jail.

Just the thought of him putting his lips on you…I really wanted that to be me. So last night, I didn't come over to my parents house to fuck you. I really came to do my normal, to protect you. And once I was there I didn't want to waste anymore time, that lil nigga was in our house and I could see, he was at you strong. But you're mine! I ain't losin' you like that; fuck that! And I know you feel the same way, I know you love me back T, you are a lot more mature than a 16 year old. Please just keep everything between us and I promise you, as soon as you turn 18, I'ma take you away from all this madness and it's gonna be just you and me. You ain't gonna want for nothin'." He leaned in a kissed me softly on my lips, my insides were starting to heat up again. I didn't want to have these feelings but I couldn't help it, he had me, and it was a wrap. A few seconds later realism set back in, and in my head all I could see is my mom. I pulled back from Whalid's soul piercing kiss and said, "What about Mom Whalid?" Before he could answer, his cell phone started ringing, he pulled the phone out of his pocket and looked at it and on the screen I could see it said, Threa. He let

it go to voicemail, but before he could even say
another word, it rang again. I said, "See how bad
karma works, answer her Whalid, we are the ones that
are wrong!"

He answered, "Hey Bae, wassup?" He paused a
moment and said, "He's right here, we're on our way
home now. Threa what's wrong…OK Babe we will hurry,
just chill out, I'll be there in a second." He hung
up the phone and turned on the car and we started out
of the parking lot, he said, "Something is wrong; I
don't know what it is, but something is wrong. We
gotta get home. But don't worry, you and I are not
done, we won't ever be done Boo-Bear." He looked over
and cracked a little grin. Reluctantly I looked at
his beautifully inviting mouth and gave him a return
grin. He reached over and lifted my t-shirt and
softly rubbed my belly button ring and said, "I love
this, it's sexy as hell, I'ma get you a diamond letter
T to go in there. Marking my shit, ya know." I
chuckled and pushed his hand down off my navel. He
ran his hand down between my legs and said, "I know
you don't wanna get me started touching you lower, we
may never get home." I smacked his hand from off of

me, he took it and put it in own his lap, pushing down on his business and said, "Down boy, T and ready to see you again right now!" He started laughing and I said, "Whatever man."

We pulled up to the house and my mom was standing on the porch crying and talking to two policemen, I didn't even notice the police cars when we pulled up. Whalid jumped out of the car quickly and said, "T stay seated Baby, don't move." He ran up onto the porch and mom collapsed in his arms. He was speaking to the police and I couldn't hear crap, the suspense got to be too much, I got out of the car and started toward the steps. Whalid looked over and yelled, "I told you to stay in the car!" I could hear more clearly mom was babbling something about why and who did this?

The policemen asked who I was, Whalid told them and they continued on to explain that early this morning one of my brother's girlfriends named Fatima called in to a 911 operator and said she had just walked in and found my brother's dad laying face down on the floor in the livingroom of my brother's home. Apparently he had been shot multiple times in his back. She was pretty badly shaken so she went out on the porch and sat until the police showed up, she told

the officer that she hadn't been able to reach my

brother all last night and that they were supposed to

be hooking up. She said that it was not out of

character for him, she knew that she wasn't his main

girl and sometimes he did these disappearing acts.

She said she decided to just show up this morning and

the door was unlocked, but didn't look as though

anyone broke in. And that's when she seen Edward's

pops on the floor. As the authorities continued to

search the home they did discover my brother's dead

body on the floor upstairs about a foot from his

bedroom. They think he was trying to get to his room,

they stated that it looked like he could go to war

with all the fire power they found in that room. And

of course, they found a ridiculous amount of drug

paraphernalia but no drugs inside of the home. He had

been out of his dad's house for about three or four

months and had rented this place. We knew nothing

about it; Ed talked mostly to TriAnn. She said she

didn't even know that he had moved away from his dad's

house.

The next few hours seemed to move in slow motion, like I was in a daze, I couldn't believe this was happening to us, but mom always said this type of thing was possible, but I never thought we would go through this. The house was filled with neighbors and family members offering their help and sorrow for our loss. And a lot of them were just being down right nebby. I went and locked myself in my room, I couldn't stand it anymore, I don't know what I was feeling. I had a lot on my plate, and though I was grieving my brother's death, I couldn't get my own twisted triangle of deceit out of my head. My world was changing it seemed moment to moment and I was getting just a little scared.

<u>Funeral Festivities</u>

The process of putting together the funeral was a really draining experience for my mom, which kind of took a toll on Whalid as well. He was right there by her side every step of the way. Whalid didn't really have any specific feelings toward Edward. He didn't have any issues with him, though he knew that Ed didn't want him with our mom. But like I said Whalid really stepped up like he should have to help mom through this time.

The person that had the most problems with this situation was TriAnn, her and Ed were very close. I thought at one point she was going lose her mind, she would be crying and then she would start babbling on and you couldn't really understand what she was saying. I just kind of stayed clear of her, I didn't want to give her any reason to snap at me. You know it seems like I'm always a sitting duck for her kicks and punches when anything is wrong. I did notice that Whalid was really helpful with her as well. He would catch her in her collapses, and there were many. He also would talk to her in the midst of her babble; telling her that Ed is in a better place now and it hurts for us now but it will get easier, that we just need to hold tight to each other at this time. She would actually calm down when he dealt with her, nobody else could seem to get through to her. That's not surprising though, he has such a soothing effect to his voice and his mannerism, he just draws you in and you feel safe.

Whalid did manage to make time for me as well, I kept telling him that I was ok. He said I was making him nervous, because I wasn't really showing a lot of emotion and usually I am so emotional. But, I didn't feel like they did, I didn't feel a need to fall out on the floor. I was sad, but that's about as far as it went. I had so many other things on my mind, I was feeling so guilty about the situation with me and Whalid. The strange thing is it didn't seem to be bothering him at all. Could all the things he said be true and he is just so into me that his conscious is untapped? I have a hard time believing it all, I think he's just busy dealing with mom and hasn't had time to deal with his guilt for these last two days.

This evening will be the viewing of my brother's body and then tomorrow will be the funeral proceedings. I'm really sick of this whole process, all the hugs and kisses and people over at our house, the house has been full every night. I spend a lot of my time in my room, I've been mostly talking to Jay-Jay and ducking calls from Mike. Periodically Whalid does stick his head in and blows kisses and such, which just keeps my mind spinning, I don't know why I can't just shake him off. I would love to tell Jay-Jay about my current situation, but I know I have to sit through this on my own.

I got my self dressed and looked over at the
clock it was 4:22pm, we were planning to leave at
4:30pm. I had on a white button up shirt with a black
tie and black slacks with a pair of Stacy Adams
loafers. I looked about as masculine as possible for
me. Naturally this is all stuff that my mom had
picked out. I looked at the boring outfit and said,
"Goodbye Eugene; hello Topaz." I hurried and changed
my shirt to a really sharp black fitted button up
shirt that Mike had made me with the matching tie.
The fabric had a slight hint of shimmer to it and you
could see through it if you looked really closely. It
wasn't overly feminine, but it did have a hint of
couture to it. I went back to the mirror quickly to
take in my look, and said, "Ahhh, now that's better."
Looking good always lifts my spirits, because God
knows I was really all crapped out on fake smiles this
week, I needed a little something to help me through
this fiasco.

I ran down the steps and met everyone at the
door, the first eyes that set on me was my Uncle Joe,
he said, "That's what I'm talkin' 'bout, you look
sharp as hell neph'. You got dat shit down, shiiit!"

I smiled and said, "Thanks Unc'." My mother looked back at me and said, "That is not what I had out for you to wear, go change that shit right now!" I looked at her and said, "Nah ma, it can't happen today, this is what I'm wearing and ain't nothing wrong with it." She turned around and marched toward me screaming, "Who the fuck are you talkin' to, I said change that shit right the fuck now before I beat the shit outta you!" I stood still in my spot, for some reason I was so unbothered by her display. I stood my ground and said, "Mom if you can give me a good reason why this shirt and tie is not ok, I'll change it but if not, I like it and I'm wearing it." She said, "I'll give your Bitch-ass a reason Muthafucka!" She grabbed me by my tie and punched me dead square in the mouth twice. I was in shock, I don't know what hurt more the hits or the comment. A hush fell over the room, I could immediately feel my top lip beginning to swell. Everyone was just standing around looking, I was so embarrassed, but that emotion faded quickly and turned into an immense anger. I did not move, I just stood there staring at my mother, to which she said, "Oh, muthafucka, you still ain't goin to take that faggotty-bullshit off, I'll fuckin' kill you, standing in my face lookin' at me like you wanna do somethin' to me, you fuckin' Bitch!" She grabbed hold to my shirt and began to tear into the fabric, you could hear it ripping as the fibers dug into my skin. I was trying to get loose from her grip when I heard TriAnn yell out, "Fuck dat faggot up ma, I'm sick of him always embarrassing us, I'm sick of it!" And within seconds I felt like I was reliving the 4th of July, I was back on the floor being beaten and choked yet again. Only difference was, this time it was mom and it was the livingroom floor. I heard Whalid yell out, "Threa no!" But before he could get to us chairs had been knocked over and a lamp had been overturned. The family members were scattering like roaches when the lights are turned on in the middle of the night. My Uncle Joe moved like the wind, he grabbed my mom off of me as I was crawling trying to get away from her. I would never hit my mom; I just wanted to get away from her. She had a death grip on my tie and was choking me big time, as my uncle was getting her off of me, TriAnn had come around and got into the scuffle, she was screaming at my uncle to let go of my

mom. Whalid dropped to his knees on the floor and put
his hands in between my neck and the grip my mom had
on the tie, which loosened the pressure. It's a good
thing, I felt like I was getting ready to pass out.
As Whalid and my Uncle Joe got my mom off me, TriAnn
took her high heel and stomped me in my back and then
kicked me in the head, and yelled, "I fuckin' hate
you, you dick-suckin' faggot!" I can't explain the
next moments, all I know is the wind that my Uncle Joe
was moving with, got underneath him again and all I
saw was TriAnn fall to the floor with an incredible
deafening thud. She was totally taken off guard by
the blow she received, but she jumped up quickly and
charged at my uncle. It was an unsuccessful lunge,
within seconds he had a death grip around her neck and
just held her still while choking her, she couldn't
move. The room was at a standstill once again;
everybody knows that my Uncle Joe is not to be fooled
with, and no one was willing to jump on him, they all
began begging for him to let her loose. My mom was
screaming and crying to my grandma, "Mama make him
stop, make him stop!" My grandma yelled, "Joseph
Bailleau take your hands off of her NOW!!!!!" He

never took his eyes off of TriAnn, his eyes were so empty and scary looking. Then he said, "You fuckin' lil' Bitch, I've told you in the past to keep your muthafuckin' hands off my baby, didn't I. Yeah and I heard about that shit you did the other day, and now it's time to pay. Bitch you like showin' out, show the fuck out on me - Bitch, I'll rip your muthafuckin' throat out!" Whalid leaped up and stood very close to my Uncle and said, "Joe man, please don't do this, I know how you feel, I know, but please, she is your niece, she's your sister's only daughter. You know I got mad respect and love for you dog, just let her go, man. This ain't you, this ain't you." I was so surprised when my uncle let TriAnn go, it was like the words that Whalid was saying pierced straight through the anger my uncle had and tapped into his soul and got him back on track. TriAnn fell to the floor like a bag of dirty laundry, she was rubbing her throat and trying to catch her breath. My mom ran over and tried to console her, then she yelled at my uncle, "Fuck you Joey, fuck you, don't touch my baby, you don't ever touch her, I'll never forgive you!!!!!" He turned his anger right back at mom and said, "You worrying about her Threa, who's goin' worry about your ass, cause if you ever do this bullshit that you just did again, Bitch I'll kill your ass!!!!!" My grandmother walked over and said, "Joe leave, NOW!!!!!" My uncle said, "I'm leavin' Mama, but I ain't playin', I'll take these muthafuckas out. Whalid man, I'ma go dog, but take care of my son, promise me man, promise me. They got me fucked up, the next time somebody put their hands on him up in here, I'ma run up through here like diarrhea, this whole muthafucka goin' be shitty!!!!!" Whalid said, "Joe man, I got it! We all family and we love you man; know that, you know we love you and I know you love us too!" At that moment my mom screamed, "Get out Joe, get the fuck out of my house!" My uncle hung his head and stomped to the door, he still had his fists balled up. When my uncle goes off it is just down right creepy, that's why everybody usually tries to avoid it, because it is very hard to calm him down.

Whalid walked over and knelt down and grabbed my grandma's hand and said, "Mrs. Bailleau, can you please take care of Threa and TriAnn, and I'll go see about Baby Boy?" My grandmother said, "Thank you

Baby, that's a great idea, and let's hurry up, we're gonna be late as hell." Whalid nodded and said, "Yes ma'am!" Whalid stood up, walked over and grabbed my hand and walked me up to my room. He shut the door behind us, and then he helped me to take off the now demolished shirt and tie. He was growling standing behind me saying, "This shit's gotta stop, I ain't gonna have it, look at this shit, what the fuck!" He leaned over and kissed me on the back of my neck and said, "Stay right here Boo-Bear, don't move." I said, "OK." He ran out the door and down the hallway, I heard him telling my grandma to go ahead and head out to the funeral home. He told her I had a deep gash in my back that was probably going to need stitches, so he was going to take me over to the Emergency Room. I heard my grandma say, "God bless you Whalid, what would we do without you. I can't stand this I got one grandbaby laying in a casket and one on the way to the hospital. What you goin' do now Lord, I can't take this!" I was making my way to my mirror on the back of my door, I didn't even realize I was bleeding, I felt the stinging but I didn't realize there was blood too. As I looked, it was pretty bad, there was blood

all over my pants and everything, it was just a damn
mess. As I looked in disgust I heard my mom telling
Whalid, "I want you with me, he can wait." To which
Whalid replied, "Theresa, you can't be serious, that
is your baby, he is your youngest child." She said,
"Fuck him, they killed the wrong one! He's the one
that I could've done without! I'm sick of this shit,
I'm tired of pretending, I hate him - I hate him - I
really do. And fuck you Whalid, you can stay here
with him and the both of you can go to hell. My son
is laying in a coffin, you can take that freak
anywhere you want to, I'm fuckin' leaving!" I felt
like a little bit of me died in that moment. Next I
heard my grandmother say, "Theresa Bailleau, you do
not mean that and you know it!" My mom replied, "Mama
I really do, I really do mean it, I'm tired of people
whispering about me and him and how he is. TriAnn is
right, it is just embarrassing." At that moment I
heard Whalid say, "You have got to be fuckin' kidding
me, what the hell are you saying. No one throws their
child away because they are not perfect in their eyes
- in God's eyes, he is perfect Threa, he is exactly
how God intended him to be. You need to stop this

bullshit!" I could hear him climbing the steps and coming toward my room. My feet were planted like they had been cemented in place. I had a completely blank stare, I just felt so empty. It is one thing to think that she had some issues with my sexuality, but to know that she does and felt as strongly as she did, pierced me to my soul and left me numb.

Whalid walked through the door and stopped, he said, "Oh God, tell me you didn't…" I said, "Yes Whalid, I did, I heard every word. And I don't care, are you leaving with them or are you going to take me so that I can get my back together?" He replied, "Huh, quit playing, I'm not going anywhere with them, I told you, I got you, and I'm so sorry about all that T, I'm gonna fix this, I promise you, I'm gonna fix it." As he gathered white towels to place on my back, as I told him, "This is your time to step back Whalid, you can't fix this. And I don't need it fixed, I am done with it!" With a puzzled look on his face, Whalid said, "What do you mean Baby? How can you be done with it, this is your family we're talking about." I turned and looked him straight in the eye and said, "You call that a family?"

I didn't speak another word all the way to the Emergency Room, while Whalid kept speaking about the importance of family and that this was all grief speaking, after the first ten or so minutes I tuned him out. As we pulled into the hospital's parking area, I released my seat belt and reached over to let myself out of Whalid's SUV, he grabbed my arm and said, "Did you hear anything that I have said Topaz?" I looked at him and said very smugly, "Sure I did Whalid. Didn't you hear me ignoring you?" I could tell he didn't know rather he should be mad at that comment or not. I said, "Thank you for bringing me, it won't be necessary for you to stay, I'm ok. I'll see you back at home, you need to go to the funeral home and be with my Mother and her dead son. Whalid got out of the truck and said, "Are all of you going crazy tonight?" I said, "Absolutely not, I'm just playing catch up." I proceeded across the parking lot and into the entrance, I heard Whalid's cell phone ringing, he said, "Go ahead T, it's my mom, I'll be right in." I didn't even turn around or respond.

Three hours and seven stitches later I was ready to be released, Whalid was sitting right there in the waiting area with his arms crossed and he had dozed off. I stood in front of him and cleared my throat, he opened his eyes and said, "Is everything OK?" I said, "Everything is fantastic, and since you didn't leave, would you mind giving me a ride home?" He looked at me and said, "Stop it, what is this. You are scaring me, it's like I did something to you, and all I did was try to protect you T." I tilted my head slightly to the right and said, "I know Boo-Bear, and I thank you for that, but I would really like to go home now if that's ok with you." I started toward the exit and Whalid followed shaking his head in confusion. He offered to help me get in the truck, I said, "That won't be necessary, I can handle it, I can handle all of this, thank you Mr. Jesper, you are such a gentleman." He got into the driver seat and said, "I don't know what the hell went on back in that Emergency Room but you are scaring me Topaz, talk to me. Baby you can tell me whatever is on your mind, I told you, I got you, but you've got to trust me." I replied with another slight head tilt, "I do trust you and you have no reason to be alarmed. You said that you've got me and I hope you don't prove yourself to be a liar, but we'll see, now won't we." He started the truck and we headed for home, it was a complete quiet ride and I could tell he was a little nervous about what was to come.

As we pulled up to the house, I could see all the cars of family and friends around our place, the house was packed again. Whalid turned the car off and said to me, "Let me go in first and see what's going on Baby and then I'll come back and get you, it'll take just a few seconds Boo, I promise." I sat up straight, turned my head to him and said, "Mr. Jesper, that won't be necessary, I live here too, remember." I got out of the SUV and proceeded across the walkway and up the front steps to the porch. Whalid was walking quickly behind me saying, "T wait, just wait a minute!" I ignored him and kept it moving. I opened the door and the room fell silent upon the sight of me. My grandma said, "How you feeling Baby?" I looked at her and tilted my head to the right and said, "Thank you for asking Mrs. Bailleau, I've never felt better." I walked straight into the kitchen where my mom and TriAnn were sitting at the kitchen table amongst about another fifteen people who were

standing and sitting around, they both had smug looks
on the faces. You could tell there was no remorse for
any of the actions that had transpired earlier. I
reached into the fridge, grabbed a bottled water and
said, "Everyone, thanks coming by and I will see you
all at the funeral tomorrow morning. Good night all."
And with a tilt of my head, I walked toward the
kitchen doorway which was being blocked by Whalid's
body, I stopped and said, "Mr. Jesper." I looked up
at him and the puzzled look on his face. He slid out
of the way so I could get by, and I said, "Thank you
Sir." And I proceeded down the hallway and up the
steps toward my bedroom. As I was moving I could hear
the whispers, "What the hell was that?" "What is the
head thing about?"

I said to myself, "Patience grasshoppers, you
will all understand soon enough." I locked my bedroom
door behind me. I sat on my bed for a minute, I was
so tired and my body was really sore. I went into my
bathroom and showered and changed my bandages on my
back, what a pain that was. I then layed across my
bed naked and told myself, "I'll get some pajamas on
in a second." The next thing I knew I was being

awaken by a light knocking on my bedroom door, I looked at the clock and it was 3:30am. I walked over to the door and said, "Yes." A whisper came from the hallway, "It's me T, please open the door." I started over toward my dresser to get something to put on and then I thought about it, and went back over to the door and said, "What Whalid?" He said, "Please T." I cracked the door just enough that he could see my face, he said, "Can I please come in?" I opened the door and said, "C'mon." He looked me over and said, "What are you doing in here?" I said, "What difference does it make are you coming in or not?" He came in and I locked the door behind him. He said, "No T, seriously, what are you doing you never walk around naked." I said, "Well, things change." As his stare was locked on me, he sat on the edge of my bed, he had his normal bed clothes on, pajama bottoms and a tank top. I walked over to the bed and said, "Now here we go; you woke me up at damn near four in the morning, what do you want Whalid?" He said, "I want to talk to you." I walked over and reached my hand down between his legs and said, "Your body doesn't seem to want to do any talking, and neither do I, I'm all talked out." I proceeded to climb into his lap and stuck my tongue into his ear, moments later we were both naked and going at it. When the deed was done, we both got into my shower and got cleaned up. He helped me to change my bandages and then he softly kissed my back and said, "I'm sorry Love, I never want to see you hurt like this again, it's driving me crazy." I kissed him on his lips and said, "I know, but I'm ok, trust me." I took his hand and led him toward the door, and said, "Back to your quarters Mr. Jesper, Topaz needs rest, tomorrow is a very busy day, as I stood behind him, I reached around him and rubbed his belly button as I place one soft kiss on the middle of his back. I then softly pushed him into the hallway and closed and locked my door. He whispered, "I love you T," I replied, "I know you do."

The morning came so quickly, I got up and began to get dressed. I was a little anxious for the day, what would today be like? I finished getting dressed and took a look in the mirror and said, "Boring…" I was in a black suit, white shirt and black tie. When I got to the bottom of the steps everyone seemed so relieved that there was no antics about what I was

wearing. I made my way out to the family limousine
thinking to myself, "How shallow and useless are these
bastards. Family, yeah right." Everything went
really smoothly getting to the church, I was pretty
quiet the whole ride over to the church, I didn't
speak a word to my mom or TriAnn. As we were getting
ready to get out of the limousine at the church,
Whalid said, "Baby Boy are you feeling ok?" I looked
up at him and gave a shady glance to TriAnn and my mom
and said, "Of course, I've never felt better." We got
out of the vehicle and made our way into the church,
the sanctuary was overrun with people. My whole
family was led by the ushers up to the first few pews
to be seated. Very early into the proceedings TriAnn
was getting started with her breakdowns. The whaling
was pretty low and the more we went on the louder it
became, at first I thought it was authentic, but as we
moved forward you could tell she was really raising
the bar.

Once we got to the point in the ceremony that the
immediate family members got the chance to say a few
words about Edward I could feel my stomach drop. One
after another the members of the family said nice

things about my brother and really painted him as the absolute picture of a saint. As it went on I started to get irritated, I just thought about how I have been so ridiculed for being gay and not bothering anyone and here we are in a packed house telling stories about an undeniable drug dealer and gangbanger. Are you kidding me, I could feel the evil churning in my core. Next up was TriAnn, I thought to myself, "And now the drama begins." My sister approached the pulpit in her black long dress, boobs pushed to the ceiling and blond weave accenting her own long jet black hair. I have to say she was done, she really did look nice. She had on a pair of five inch heels similar to the ones that she left this gash in my back with last night. She made it up to the microphone with the help of Whalid, who was the perfect gentleman. She was kind of hanging all over him, he stood back while she spoke, just in case she decided to fall out, we all know her well. She began by saying, " Edward I miss you so much!" She then began down this road of when they were kids and life was so good and how close they remained and she went on about how she will never feel whole again. She then began screaming and shouting and jumping up and down, all an

act I can assure you. Anytime we went to church,

TriAnn ran up and down the aisles and such, it's just

how she gets down. So today, she was really in full

concert mode, when I looked up again her shoes were

off and she was pacing back and forth in the pulpit,

shouting, "Why Eddie, why did you have to leave me!"

Whalid came over and put his arm around her and she

began to breakdown on him, it was so messy, I could

hardly hold in my laughter. Then she walks back to

the microphone and says, "Thank y'all for celebrating

the life of the king of our family, my brother Edward

Bailleau. There will never be another. It's just you

and me Ed, like it's always been, just you and me!

And now I'm all alone. Oh God, I can't - I don't know

what I'm gonna do without my bro. I love you Ed!"

Whalid went to get her down from the pulpit, it was

just getting to be to much. I felt the little dig

that was thrown by her, like my mom only had them two,

but I was like, "Whatever, she's a mess." But before

TriAnn left the pulpit she stood back at the mic and

said, "I have one last thing I'd like to say, Mama

thank you for giving me one brother, that I loved with

all my heart, it's the one thing you did do right!"

Oh my goodness, there was a moment there where I swear

you could hear the gasp through the church and then it

was followed by complete silence. I almost died

laughing, if you could've seen my mother's face, she

was in shock. The two of them had been getting along

so good lately; they had something in common, they had

both been abusing me. But that just goes to show,

there is no honor amongst thieves, and that's just how

TriAnn is, the only person sacred to her was now lying

in the beautiful box. I didn't care about her

denouncing me, and I definitely didn't feel sorry for

mom, I felt like she somewhat deserved it, Lord knows,

she had been dishing grief my way all week. What

comes around, goes around. By this time my

grandmother had motioned for Whalid to get TriAnn out

of the pulpit and he did. One of the mothers of the

church took over the service, she began praying and

really regained control over the church. Then she

motioned to me to come up, it was my turn to speak.

As I started toward the pulpit, my stomach felt

nauseas, but I kept it moving. I stepped behind the

microphone and before I ever got to say a word, TriAnn

shouted out, "Nobody wants to hear what you have to say, just get down and go away!" She was no longer sitting beside my mom, she was a little further down the pew. My mom was crying and looking as though she was in agreement. I just stood there for a moment, the church was quiet. I looked at Whalid sitting next to my mother, he mouthed silently, "Go ahead Baby." I put my head down, Whalid stood up and came to the pulpit, he got behind me and whispered in my ear, "You got this, say what's on your heart Love, I got you, no matter what, remember that." I put my head up and said, "OK, everyone, sorry for the slight hold up, this is really an emotional time for me and my family." I was then interrupted by TriAnn's shrieking voice, "Ed didn't like you either, he don't want you saying nothing over him, about him, to him or nothin', just go away, we all hate you and don't want you in this family." I seen my Uncle Joe stand up and move toward the pulpit, I thought to myself, "Oh boy, here we go!" I stood still in my spot, I could feel the anger building in my core. I tilted my head slightly to the right and before I could say a word, I heard Whalid whisper, "No T, please." I chuckled to myself and thought, "He's catching on, smart man." I then

proceeded and said, "I thank you all for stomaching

the TriAnn Show. She hasn't been well groomed, but I

am sure you have picked up on that by now. I wanted

to say a few words about my brother who is lying here,

is that so terrible?" TriAnn jumped up from her pew

and screamed, "Everything about you is terrible, you

freak! You need to go somewhere." She looked over at

my mother and said, "Why don't you sit your friendly

neighborhood fag down somewhere, I'm so sick of this."

My mom stood up and said, "Eugene, she's right we

don't want to hear it, just sit down!" My grandmother

motioned for Whalid to bring me away from the pulpit.

I turned to him and said, "Don't get caught up in

their mess, because I am not feeling this today!"

Whalid stepped back, Uncle Joe said, "I'm going to go

off if anyone else says anything to him before he is

done, I promise y'all - there won't be another prayer

said up in here!" I said, "Thanks Uncle Joe, I love

you so much, and folks I'm sorry for this ridiculous

display of foolishness. The only thing I would like

to say is rest in peace Ed, you are lucky, you don't

have to fight for your place anymore, you don't have

to fight for anyone to love you. Though you weren't always nice, God forgives and I know he came and got you. I pray you followed him to the promise land. I don't know how you felt totally about me but I did love you sincerely, my big brother." At that moment one tear ran down my cheek as I began to leave the pulpit. TriAnn shouted, "He didn't love you, you nasty faggot!!!!!" She kicked off her shoes and charged directly for me. Before she could get her hands on me my Uncle Joe had jumped in front of me, the force of her charging made him lose his footing and he and TriAnn barreled into the coffin. It shook fiercely and with a loud slam the top closed with incredible force, as all of the flowers fell off onto the floor. My mom leaped up and screamed, "NO, NO, NO, NO, NO!!!!!" My uncle had risen to his feet by this time and TriAnn was screaming, "You don't have nothin' to do with it, you loser!" You could see Uncle Joe trying to hold it together, my grandmother was on her knees on the floor praying and crying. Uncle Joe said, "TriAnn go away please, I swear to The All-Mighty if you say another word to me, I'ma put some hair on the wall up in here!" Whalid quickly grabbed my uncles arm, "Joe man, not here, not here,

man." He looked and Whalid and said, "I know man,

I'm out!" He started toward the door. By this time

the preacher had gotten to the pulpit and said, "Let's

all be seated, in the Lord's house." My mom said,

"TriAnn what is it gonna take before you stop!!!!!"

TriAnn looked at mom and said, "Shut up, you don't

have nothin' to say. You can't do nothin' right.

It's your fault that he is in that coffin, if you had

never thrown him out, this wouldn't have happened!"

Mom said, "Shut your mouth right now, you ungrateful,

yellow Bitch! I've done all I could for y'all

muthafuckas and you'rr still not satisfied. What the

fuck do you want from me?" TriAnn screamed back, "I

don't want nothin' from your trick-ass, and you're

another yellow Bitch! And if you keep talkin' I

swear…" Mom moved like a bolt of lightning, she was

out of her shoes and on TriAnn like flies on dog mess.

She had TriAnn by the hair and was just steadily

banging her in the face, jewelry was flying off

everywhere. The quickness of mom's attack caught

TriAnn off-guard; TriAnn outweighs mom by a lot, but

it wasn't helping. Mom's hands were moving like

machinery and she was connecting with every hook and jab. My grandmother ran in between the two of them and before she could get order, TriAnn had regained her footing and now she had knocked mom's hat off and gotten a death grip in mom's hair and with my grandmother in the middle the tussle toppled over with such a force that the three of their bodies literally had knocked the casket completely over onto the church floor. It was totally on its side and through a slight opening of the lid you could see my brother's hand hanging out onto the floor. I was mortified at the sight of it, this was just awful. I couldn't move, and as Whalid went to move toward the commotion, his dad had come to the front of the church and grabbed him by the arm and told him, "Son, sometimes you just can't. I won't allow you to be in harm's way under these circumstances." As I seen Whalid being pulled away by Mr. Jesper, I felt a slight tug to my arm, it was Mrs. Jesper, she said, "Sweet Baby, you've suffered enough, come with me." I obeyed and followed the Jesper family toward the door as my family scrapped and rolled about on the church floor like animals. As we were going down the church steps, the police were coming up the steps. I just thought to

myself, "How ridiculous and what a circus."

Separation Can Be Good

We got outside to where the Jesper's had their car parked, Mrs. Jesper told me to get inside and have a seat. I said, "Yes ma'am," as I opened the door I could feel my cell phone vibrating in my pocket. I took it out and looked at it, it was Jay-Jay, the text said, "Chile, what's going on, my gram heard something on her scanner!" His grandmother was a nebby older woman that was always sitting by that scanner listening for everytime the cops left the station, my goodness. I decided I would text him later with the details. A few seconds later I heard Whalid say, "Are you kidding me?" I looked out of the window in disbelief, as the police were escorting my mom and my sister out of the church in handcuffs; I was done. I didn't know whether to laugh or cry, this was total embarrassment at it's best. And just when you thought it couldn't get any better, out of the corner of my eye I seen a van pull up, and then another; you have got to be kidding me. It is Channel 11 and Channel 4, I slid down in the seat, I was absolutely mortified.

I cracked the car door open and said, "Mrs. Jesper can we go? I don't care where, just anywhere but here." She said, "Sweet Baby, you're so right." She looked over at Mr. Jesper and said, "Wade let's go." Without a second thought he opened her car door and waited for her to be seated, he proceeded to the driver side and sat down; and rolled his window down and told Whalid, "Son, get in, now is not the time to be the hero, this is a bit too messy, you got too much to lose!" Whalid nodded his head and said, "Yes Sir." Whalid jumped in the back seat with me, and we were off. As we sat in the back seat I was quiet and so was everyone else in the car, Whalid put his hand on my knee and said, "It's OK T, it will all work out. You'll see, I know it's all messed up and confusing right now, but that's how life is sometimes, you know I love you right." I shook my head yes and just looked out the window. After a brief silence Mrs. Jesper said, "Whalid I am so proud of you, do you know that. You are a stand up man for Theresa and I know you want to be there for her, but this is a serious family matter and you aren't married, nor are you the father of the children, this is why we insisted that you did not get in the middle, because I know she loves you, but your standpoint is not always valid when it comes to matters of a family that was started without you, so it is sometimes better to take two steps back, instead of one step too far in. Do you understand?" Whalid said, "Absolutely Mama." She then looked over her shoulder at me and said, "I hope you do as well Sweet Baby, we don't want you to feel as though we abandoned your mother at her time of need, but with the authorities and all of the heightened attitudes we felt it best that we go. Right now your grandmother will take care of things for your mom and she should be home within a few hours, I'm sure of it. We took you with us because, we have absolutely fallen in love with you and want to see nothing harmful come your way. I told Wade that once your Uncle Joseph had gone that I wasn't comfortable to leave you there without Whalid. I hope you understand, and I will explain everything to Theresa, she knows me and she knows I have your best interest and hand. And you are somewhat a son to Whalid, he loves you a lot, I hope you know that." I looked over at Whalid, he had a smile on his face. I softly said, "Yes ma'am, I know." While thinking, "Lady, you don't know the half

of it! I'm something to him, but I don't think it's a

son." For the next couple of hours I couldn't get an

answer from my grandmother or mom and I was starting

to get a little worried. I think Whalid noticed it

and asked his father if he would mind taking us over

to our house so that we could change our clothes and

get more comfortable, and Whalid could get his truck.

Mr. Jesper said sure, and we were out. When we got

over to the house, no one was there, so we told Mr.

Jesper we would be right back over to their house

after we changed or clothes. We decided to put the

food away that was sitting out that was meant for the

family to eat after the services. Whalid said to me

as we were putting things away, "You know what T, I

want you to pack a few outfits that will last you for

the next few days. I'm going to have you stay over at

my folks' house while we get everything straightened

out around here, and I don't want to have you here

while I'm at work 'til I know everything is chill." I

just stopped and looked at him and said, "I guess so,

if that's what you want." He said, "That's one of the

things that I want for right now," as he chuckled a

bit, I ran upstairs to pack my bag.

I was trying to get my last pair of shoes in the

bag when I was suddenly lifted off of my feet and into

the air. I said, "Boy put me down before you hurt my

back." He put me down and said, "Hurry up Babe, so we

can go, I'm a little tired." I said, "If you let me

drive, you can rest on the way back over to your

parent's house." He said, "Maybe I will, cause I

might let you drive stick later on. Would you like

that?" I gave him a dirty look and said, "Whatever,

you are so nasty, let's go!" He said, "Can I have a

kiss first?" I walked over to him with my hands full

with my bags and gave him a peck on the cheek and

said, 'Let's go; do you ever think about anything

else?" He laughed and said, "Sure I think about how

warm and tight you are, and how I can't wait to travel

your road again." I walked out of my bedroom door and

down the hallway as Whalid followed behind me. We

locked the house up, jumped in his SUV and headed out.

It seemed as though we got back to the Jesper's home

in no time. When we walked back in the house, you

could smell something that was really calling on my

hunger pains. I followed Whalid to the kitchen where
we found Mrs. Jesper cooking up a storm. She said,
"Have a seat, I'm almost done and we will all sit and
eat together." She told Whalid to go and get his
father for dinner.

As Whalid left the room she asked me, "Did I hear
Whalid refer to you as T today in the car?" I said,
"Yes ma'am, you did." She turned to me and said,
"What is that, and where'd it come from?" I replied,
"It's a nickname that he and some of my friends call
me. They call me Topaz, and he just shortens it to T
most of the time." She sat down across from me and
said, "Topaz, oh I love that Sweet Baby, and it really
fits you. You are such a gorgeous young man with such
a sweet soul. Topaz is my favorite stone, it's
breathtaking, just like you. Do you mind if I call
you that too? I really like that, oh yeah." I said,
"That is fine by me, I really don't like Eugene, and I
never have." At that moment Whalid walked back into
the kitchen and sat down, he said, "What y'all talkin'
about?" His mom said, "Topaz," she was sitting there
with a large grin on her face. Whalid was looking
like he just swallowed a piece of gum he'd been

chewing. Mrs. Jesper continued, "You know how I love topaz, and I was just saying how gorgeous he is, just like the stone. Oh, wait a minute, you didn't tell me where you got it from or why you chose that Sweet Baby." Whalid chimed in, "I named him that ma, like you said it just kind of fit him." She just smiled and starting singing as she began to prepare our plates. Whalid looked at me and smiled and then said, "Ma, don't let T fool you and get you all wrapped around his finger." At that instance, you could hear an equally as deep voice coming from the hallway, "He has become such a part of this family already, it's nice having some life other than me and mom around here, you're always welcome Lil Man!" and with that Mr. Jesper came over and gave me a hug. The Jespers are so much opposite my family that is sometimes kind of scary. They make me feel so at home and so safe.

Around 9:30pm Mr. and Mrs. Jesper and I were sitting around in the gameroom on the bottom floor of the home, I could see them dosing off a little while I was so engulfed in the vampire flick we were watching. Whalid was making calls trying to get information on my family's whereabouts. He came down the steps and said, "Looks like their holding them, they will most likely be out tomorrow. So we are both gonna stay over here tonight." Mrs. Jesper said, "I think that's for the best, Topaz baby, don't worry it's gonna be alright. Whalid, you get him everything he needs for the guest room, me and dad are going up, you know we are way past our time of slumber," she chuckled. Whalid said, "Yeah the two of them are usually in their room by 8 o'clock every night," he laughed and said, "He ain't gotta stay in the guest room, he ain't a guest he can sleep in my room, we will watch movies and make popcorn and stuff, it'll be like a slumber party." The Jesper's both laughed and Mrs. Jesper said, "Topaz, baby we tried to get him to grow up but he just won't, slumber parties at 27; that's my baby. We will see you guys in the morning, good night." We said, "Good night," as they climbed the stairs. No sooner than I could hear them get to the top of the second floor staircase I punched Whalid in the chest softly and said, "Slumber party, you are so corny." He said, "I'm not corny, I'm just fucked up over this lil' nigga I know wit little hands and feet, a flat stomach and a killer ass. He got some fire ass lips,

and he smells like baby lotion and baby powder all the
time. And he taste like he bathes in whip cream.
Look what happens when I even think about my boo." He
lifted his shirt to expose the obvious rise in his
nature. I just laughed a bit and said, "You stupid,
man." He slid over close to me and said, "Touch it,
c'mon T, touch it, you did it. Now you gotta touch it
for me, I love the feel of your little ass hands
around my microphone, it drives me crazy." He took my
hand and put it in his lap, I turned my head and acted
like I was really so into the movie, even though I
really wasn't at that point. I could feel myself
starting to slip into his grasp as usual. I took my
hand off of his now throbbing knot of flesh in his
jeans and said, "You love my touch, but who is that
other sissy you were describing?" I laughed and
crossed my legs into a pretzel and sat on my feet in
the corner of the huge love seat we were on. He slid
over and put his hand up my shirt and started
caressing my nipple and saying, "You know who I'm
talkin' about, and I don't know why you makin' me beg,
but if that's what you want. I'll beg for that ass
everyday." I could feel myself weakening so I jumped

up off the couch and humerously said, "What you mean man, I ain't wit that shit, you want this ass you goin' have to take it my dude." I could hardly hold my laugh in, Whalid backed up and said, "Oh now you hard, or are you makin' fun of me?" I said, "No my dude, aint nothin' funny, and you the one that's all hard and shit, punk." Whalid started to laugh as he tackled me and wrestled me to the floor, he was cracking up laughing as he kept pinning me into different sexual positions and saying, "Do you give." I would say, "Never," and wiggle out of it, which was kind of easy with me being so small. He tried to get me one time and tripped on his own foot and fell, I jumped on his back as he was face down on the floor. I straddled him right at his lower back and grabbed his butt cheeks with both hands and said, "Let's see how you like it, your always rubbing on my ass like it's some kind of crystal ball or something." He didn't say anything at first, but when one of my fingers accidentally slid and rolled down along his crack, he grabbed my hand and said, "OK T, playtime is over, that ain't no good look Babe." I jumped up and said, "I'm sorry, I didn't mean to…" he said, "I know

you didn't, and I ain't mad, but I ain't made that
way." I laughed at him and tackled him to the floor
and straddled his stomach, it is so much fun to jump
all over him, because there is so much of him and it
is all milk chocolate in color and rock hard. I
pushed his shirt up and said, "Well what about this,
does this make you nervous too?" I ran my finger
across his nipple, then ran my hand down his sculpted
stomach, he gasped for some air, as I licked his belly
button one time very lightly. The rise in his jeans
was back almost instantaneously, which made me
chuckle. I then sat up on him and asked him had he
ever heard the expression, "Save a horse and ride a
cowboy." He said, "No, and where the hell did you
hear it," I said, "Again, you ain't with me 24 hours a
day, lil' dude. Now just be patient and if you play
your cards right, later on I show you how it works."
He began begging again for me to touch his microphone.
I said, "What is your fascination with my music Mr.
Jesper?" He said, "I love the way you sing!" As he
lay on his back on the floor of the gameroom, I gave
in to his request and told him hand me the mic, to
which I fiercely performed an A and B selection, if

you know what I mean. He enjoyed the flow of my
performance until his juke box was absolutely out of
coins.

I sat up on the couch and went back to watching a
now new movie that had come on the television, and
about ten minutes later as I looked over he was
snoring and sleeping like a baby. I continued with
the movie until I eventually fell off to sleep, when I
awoke, I was being carried up the steps to the second
floor to Whalid's bedroom. I never let on that I was
awake, he laid me on the bed and sat there and looked
at me for about ten minutes. He went back and locked
the door, stood at the head of his king size bed and
stripped down naked, he then removed all my clothes
and whispered in my ear, "Are you woke Baby," I looked
over at the red digital numbers on his clock that said
2:38am, and said, "Unfortunately." He said, "That's
ok, you made a promise to me earlier and now you gotta
make good on it." He then began to service my body
like a mechanic on a brand new sportscar, every touch
was so soft and so precise, that I could hardly stay
still. Once he had me wound up to the point of no
return he said, "Now show me how you think you can

save a horse." He laid on his back and whispered,

"Wassup Baby" I whispered back, "Surely you are not

challenging me," he said, "Your lil' ass was the one

talkin' shit earlier." I looked down at him and said,

"Lights out nigga," I mounted him and it was all down

hill from there, he couldn't even form anymore words

to say to me, I was drowned in a sea of, "uh huh,"

"mmm," "yeah, yeah," "ohhh," and "der, der, der" I

covered his mouth with my hand as I finished him off

with a few last deadly glides. I got up and went to

the shower, a few minutes after I was in there he

showed up dragging along. He said, "I have to admit,

I felt like a lil' Bitch, my legs were shaking and I

couldn't stop them, I had to wait awhile before I

could get up. You got me fucked up T." Then his

kissed me long and deep as the water flowed so gently

over our heads. Everything was just so perfect in

that moment, that I had absolutely forgotten about the

embarrassment that I called my family.

When I woke up the next morning it was almost

7am, I slid out of Whalid's "It's all mine" grip, I

could immediately smell food being prepared. I went

and washed my face, brushed my teeth and put on pajama

bottoms and a t-shirt. I tip-toed out of the room closing the door behind me, I followed the food smell down to the kitchen where I found the Jespers laughing and talking like it was mid-afternoon, they were wide awake. They were so welcoming to me, I sat and had breakfast with them, they never brought up anything about the craziness of my family, I mean, they were just so respectful of my feelings. Eventually a very groggy Whalid came downstairs and joined us, after he ate and kept playing with my feet under the table, he began making phone calls to figure out what was up with my mom and sister. By 12pm he'd found out that they were both to be released around 4pm, he decided that he would pick up mom, Mr. Jesper would be picking up TriAnn, and I would stay put. I just did as I was told, Whalid said he wasn't chancing any of my safety, he wanted to know exactly what everyone was thinking before I would be around them.

Well me staying put ended up turning into a four day excursion, I had been with the Jespers for almost a full week and though I was loving all the attention I didn't want to wear out my welcome. Whalid had been by the house a few times, but never more than twenty

minutes. He brought me money and he would text me, so
I didn't feel thrown away, but what were we doing
here. I hadn't spoken to any of my family, Jay-Jay
was telling me about all the talk in the streets about
the news coverage of the funeral, and how it had
really shook the family name a bit. That evening I
talked to Whalid for a few moments and told him, "I
can't just stay here like this, I've got to come
home." He said, "No problem, when I get from work,
I'll come by and get you." I was all packed up and
ready to go when Whalid showed up after work. I gave
my thanks and said goodbye to the Jespers and we were
out.

"So, how is she Whalid? Is she stomping around
mad, is she regretting all the madness or what, what's
up?" He looked at me and said, "Man, yesterday is the
first time her and I weren't straight up arguing over
her part in that madness, and that's because I refused
to talk about it. I missed you though, I miss you
being at the house where I can see your sexy ass a
couple times a day. I started to come all the way
over to my parents' house to kiss you at like three
o'clock in the morning last night." I said,

"Whatever, then you should've, I was up!" He said, "What the hell were you doing up?" I said, "Chillin', why, I ain't ask you nothing about what you be doin' to pass the time." We were pulling up to the house, I had all intentions on talking to my mom about some of the things she had said, I thought she owed me an apology, or at least some clarification.

I walked into the house, she was sitting on the couch watching TV and looking evil, drinking a glass of soda. I sat across from her on the love seat, I said, "Mom, how are you feeling?" Her response was curt and quick, she said, "Who wants to know?" I sighed and said, "Really, are we going to do this or are we going to talk and straighten this situation out. There were some things that we need to clarify." She sat straight up, and Whalid sat down across the room in another chair. And then she began, "What do we need to clarify Gene, I said what I meant, and I meant what I said. I'm not gonna take back anything I've said. I am tired of people having something to say about you, I'm sick of it!" I sat up and said, "Mom, what do you want me to do? There's nothing that I can do about what someone wants to say about me, I mean, I'm not understanding your point." She was becoming more and more defensive. She said, "I am embarrassed by you. People are literally laughing at you and this family. It's like you are not a son, I don't know what you are." Tears were coming up to my eyes, I said, "And you even wished me dead, how could you?" She looked at me and said, "What's that faggoty- bullshit you say? It is what it is!!!!!" I was so hurt, I said, "That's it I'm sick of it, it's a no win - I'm done! Nothing I do pleases you, I go to school, make good grades, I'm respectful to you, but none of that matters. Because you are so stuck in some fantasy land where it doesn't matter if you are selling drugs, gang banging, fighting with people, or heck even fighting with you, just as long as your straight. But since I'm not, then I'm not worthy of your affection, and that is so wrong. And for you to actually say that the wrong child got killed, and you refuse to think that there is anything wrong with that. And you scream about respecting you, you have to be respectful as well." She moved to the front of her chair and yelled, "Bitch, I don't have to repect you, and I'm done with you faggot, fuck you!!!!" Then she threw her soda in my face, it went everywhere, I was so humiliated. Whalid yelled at her, "Fuck that Threa, that's some bullshit!" I was so upset, I stood up and started for the door, I heard her scream, "Yeah, get the fuck out of my house!!!!!" I stopped and turned around and said, "You know what mom, gladly, I will gladly leave from this place, you take care of yourself." I could hear her screaming as I walked off the porch, "Fuck you, and get the fuck outta my house!!!!!"

In Need of a New Start

When I stepped off of that porch, I didn't have a clue where I was going but I knew it was time for me to move on with my life without these folks. I just couldn't take another one of these episodes. I wanted to slap my mother so bad, but I would never do that, but oh how the palm of my hand itched for the connection. I just started walking, I had left the bags of clothing that I was bringing back home, all I had on me was my cell phone and $125.00 that was left of the money that Whalid had given me a few days prior. I began to cry; I didn't know what I was going to do or where I was going to go. I pulled out my phone, I was going to call Jay-Jay and see if I could crash with him tonight and then I could figure something out tomorrow, but before I even got the chance to dial the number, I could here footsteps approaching me quickly, of course it was Whalid. He said, "You moved to quickly T, why did you leave, I can fix this." I said, "Whalid, there is no fixing it, I'm done. I will never step foot back in the house again; I don't deserve this, I haven't done anything to anyone. Yet, I've had death wished upon me, I have stitches in my back. I have One-of-a-kind articles of clothing that have just been ripped to shreds, and not to mention enough embarrassment to last me the rest of my days. What more do you want, what would satisfy you, the only thing that would make them happy is me trading places with Edward and I wouldn't give them the satisfaction. I'm gonna make something of myself, they'll see! But, I don't care if I never see them again!" He grabbed me and embraced me and said, "You're angry, and you don't mean that." I said, "I do!" He said, "C'mon, I'm going to take you back over to my parents' house," I said, "No, they don't want to keep taking me in, that's ridiculous!" He just about drug me back down the street to his SUV, reassuring me that his parents are not like that, I knew it but I didn't want to keep falling back into their lap, I wasn't their responsibility. I sat in the truck with Whalid driving over to his parents' place, I thought I had pulled it together, until I was walking up their walkway and I just lost it. As I was walking up with

Whalid's arm around me, the door came open and in the

doorway like a glowing angel was Mrs. Jesper. She

said, "Whalid, I'm getting a little tired of this

now!" Then I heard Mr. Jesper's voice coming from

inside the house, "Trudy!" I broke away from Whalid's

arms and said, "I told you, I told you, why did you do

this Whalid, why?" I ran down the walkway away from

the house, he caught me before I could get out of the

gate and picked me up in a bear hug and said, "Stop it

now, and go in the house," I said, "How many houses do

you want me to be thrown out of, how many before

you're satisfied. Am I not humiliated enough for you

Whalid, then I'm sorry, I'm sorry about everything –

put me down and just let me go away before someone

else throws me away!" By this time Mrs. Jesper had

made it down to the walkway, she stood in front of me

with a stern look on her face and said, "Topaz… Topaz!

Put him down Whalid, and you stop all this talk right

now boy. There is no throw away, you take your little

self and you walk into that house, right now! Chop,

chop! We don't do public displays for the neighbors,

if they want a show they will have to go to the cinema

and pay. We are not the subjects of their laughter,

and judgment." I walked into the house, thinking, "Oh boy, where'd the nice older lady go to?" That thought was followed with, "Is she going to hit me when I get in here, or would Whalid's dad be doing the hitting now?" Either way I was scared as I crossed the door frame. Mrs. Jesper walked in behind me, she pointed to the livingroom which was on the left of the hallway and said, "Go over there and sit little boy and you too Whalid!" You could hear the elevating anger in her tone. She sat next to her husband on the couch, which was across the room from the love seat that we were sitting on. She began, "Let me tell you something, when I say something, I mean it, do you understand that! I want to make sure, because I will not revisit this conversation. I don't know how much Whalid has told you about us but we don't play. If I say that I love you, then that's it, there is nothing else. There's no I love you, except for… I don't play those kinds of games, nor do I accept that type of foolishness in my surroundings. Now, I'm going to be nice and explain what I meant by my comment, which is a stretch for me to have to explain myself to a 16 year old or the 27 year old next to you, who already knows what the comment was in reference to. I am getting tired of the way you are being treated by your family, and it is really wearing me down. I have discussed this with Whalid and my husband, to which I have been told to mind my business. Now explain to me what has gone on this time and what in the hell is that mess all over your clothes and skin." As Whalid began explaining, I sat quietly. I thought for a moment that Mrs. Jesper's eyes were going to pop right out of her head, she was furious, she looked over at Mr. Jesper and said, "Now what Wade! Now what am I to do!" He said, "Calm down Trudy, calm down." She said, "I'm tired of being calm, I should've followed my first instinct with this mess!" She stood up and began laying the laws of the land as written by Trudy Jesper. She said, "Topaz, I see you, I see you sitting here in your entirety, you are 16 years old, period. You are not an adult and I would be less than a woman to watch as you're being robbed of your innocence without at least trying to help you. You are overly mannerable, in the midst of all the fussing and cussing and fighting, I have not seen you step out of character one time, and I'm telling you a couple of those times I needed glue on the seat of my pants so that I wouldn't step out of my lane. You've been dealt a less than favorable hand, now what is it that you are to do with it? You make the best of it. You are different...And! You like boys as opposed to liking girls. Do you think that you are the only person in the world who has this going on?" I felt like I was going to faint, but I answered, "No ma'am." She said, "Does that make you a bad person, or do you feel like something is wrong with you?" I answered, "No ma'am, not at all." She continued, "You're right, it doesn't and there isn't! Now what I'm tired of, is the physical and the unnecessary verbal abuse that keeps coming your way, it is ridiculous. That's what I was talking about, when I said I was tired of this; not you being here with us. I love knowing that you are here, because that's the only time I know that no one is putting their hands and their drinks on you. So for this reason, Whalid and Wade, he is not going back and that is final!!!!! Whalid get up, go and get the guest bedroom together right now, I'm done with this. I will be setting up a little meeting with your mama, but don't worry, this is done!" No one spoke another word, it was as she said, DONE.

In the following days I was given house keys, a new cellphone(because the day after the blowup, mom cut mine off), and Whalid took me to the mall to buy all new clothes. Mrs. Jesper gave him a credit card and told him to take me and get everything I needed for now and also for the upcoming start of the school year because it would be time in less than a month. Right before we left for the mall, I was standing at the front door and I heard her instructing Whalid not to go over $2500.00 on that card and he told her that was fine, but if there was more needed that he would make up the difference on one of his cards. He also told her that I was his responsibility and that he would take over the payments on her card and promised to have it paid off within 60 days. I was dumbfounded by the generosity of both them, especially after they started debating who should pay, Mr. and Mrs. Jesper felt like it wasn't necessary for Whalid to pay, they said it was all their idea to take me on and that the cost should be theirs. Whalid disagreed, naturally, for his own reasons that were left unsaid. I really don't know what the outcome of that was, it was very nice to feel wanted by someone other than Whalid. At the mall I had a great time shopping and was almost successful in forgetting my troubles. I made the conscious effort not to be ridiculous, I just picked what I needed, just as if I didn't know about the amount of availability to shop heavily. My total for everything was under $1500.00, to which Whalid kept suggesting additional items and I kept saying no. Once we were in the car, he said to me, "T it's ok, you can have whatever you want, we have the finances to cover it, my dad has an excellent job and so does my mom, and you already know I'm good. So stop trying to hold back and let yourself be spoiled, we want to spoil you. You deserve all the love that can be poured on you." We got back to the house and I was really exhausted, yet so high on the excitement of it all. The first thing I saw when we came in was the Jespers in the livingroom; they were watching television. When they seen us, Mr. Jesper turned off the television and Mrs. Jesper said, "C'mon and show us what you got, I bet you picked out a bunch of cute stuff Topaz." But really I hadn't, I just grabbed the basics. Jeans, t-shirts, button down shirts and

Timbs, a nice pair of loafers and a pair of Nikes. We

went through the bag and immediately, I could see the

disappointment on Mrs. Jesper's face. She said, "What

is this mess, this looks like a bag of clothes that

Whalid has chosen for himself." She looked over at

Mr. Jesper and said, "Wade, I'm not going to have

this!" She looked at Whalid and said, " I know you

didn't confine him to this masculine image and try to

suppress his femininity. Cause I'm not going to have

it, my baby can dress anyway he likes. Where's all

the little tight fitted shirts and tank tops that you

love to wear, there's nothing wrong with it, it's cute

on you, and it's the way you express yourself freely,

and that's you baby." I assured her that Whalid had

nothing to do with it, and that whenever my mom sent

me shopping, I wasn't allowed to purchase anything

that she deemed as girly with her money, I had to find

a way to get it myself. Mrs. Jesper told me that I

needed to get out of that mind set and that whenever

her or her husband gave me anything it was mine to

spend how I see fit, as long as it is legal and not

harming me or someone else. Mrs. Jesper also told me

that her and mom were going to be meeting up tomorrow to talk about my situation. I got really nervous just at the mention of it, how was this going to play out. What ridiculous things will mom say that may have me thrown out of here on my ear.

The next day was a Saturday, I had butterflies in my stomach all morning, knowing that this afternoon could end up like a scene from 'The Clash of the Titans.' I was sitting on the front steps when Mr. and Mrs. Jesper were leaving to attend the lunch date with mom. I told them I would be right here when they returned, Mrs. Jesper looked at me and said, "Topaz are you feeling ok," I said, "Yes ma'am, just a little nervous, that's all." She said, "Don't be, this here is grown up business, and the grown ups are going to handle it, this is not for you to worry about, you let us worry about this." I nodded my head and smiled, as she marched off down the walkway in her high heeled sandals and black silk, one-shoulder dress, I thought to myself, "Well go on then, Grown Lady." Mr. Jesper was wearing a perfectly matching black silk shirt and a really nice pair of black slacks, with a slide on Stacy Adams shoe. They really were looking sharp, anyone would be happy to have them as parents, Whalid was really lucky.

I was enjoying myself with the house all to myself sitting on the porch playing games on my cell phone when I got a text from Whalid, that said, "I know you are home alone!" I text him back, "No I'm not!" He then text, "If I catch you in a lie do I get to have my way with you?" I text, "Go for it!" All of a sudden, the front door opens and out walks Whalid, it scared me almost half to death, I said, "How did you…" he interrupted, "I came in through the back door with my key. But you lied, and now you've got to pay up. I got something to knock all those lies out of your mouth. Hurry up, we don't have a lot of time. And I been craving you bad." I got up off the steps and went into house, he slammed and locked the door behind me and grabbed my hand and led me up the steps and into his bedroom. He kissed and stripped me quickly and without hesitation did as he said in his text. He literally had his way with me, it was the best hour I had spent in the last few days, it left my body tingling all over. Once we got cleaned up we went down to the gameroom and awaited

his parents' return to see what my mom's reaction was
to the Jesper's taking me in. As we sat there, Whalid
was his usual nasty self, licking on me and rubbing on
me every five seconds. I kept hitting him and telling
him to stop, which he wouldn't, and who am I kidding,
I really didn't want him to, I was enjoying my private
time with him just as much as he was. About another
30 minutes later we heard the opening of the front
door. We both leaped up and headed for the steps, we
met up with the Jespers in the livingroom.

    Mrs. Jesper laughed and said, "Look at my two
beautiful men. What are you two up to?" Whalid said,
"We were waiting on you, what happened, please tell me
Threa acted like she had some sense." Mrs. Jesper
said, "And why wouldn't she, I've never had harsh
words with Theresa. She was fine. Now, she was not
responsive to the harm that she has done with Topaz
and TriAnn. And I'm sorry Sweet Baby but she had no
apologies for her behavior nor did she fight to get
you back home, so just look at it as a blessing. God
has blessed you and us with a brand new start. I told
her I would take full care of Topaz and she was free
to, "Do her," as she says. She was ok with the idea,

so Topaz you still got your mama, she's not going anywhere, and give her time, things will most likely change. But until that time you have gained two people who love, and adore you." Whalid chimed in, "And you already had me!" Mr. Jesper stood up and said, "I'm so glad all this mess is behind us, Whalid go and get some glasses, we're gonna have a toast." Whalid came back with a glass of wine for each of them and a glass of ginger ale for me and we toasted. Mr. Jesper led us in the toast, he said, "Through a stormy time, light has been shined onto this home once again. Lil' Man, may it be as much a blessing to you as you are to us, we love you, and welcome to your new home Son!"

Reunification Possibilities

Although everything was ideal at my new home with the Jespers there was a small part of me that actually missed my own family, again I was probably being a little naïve. This part of me that longed to belong

and be accepted by my biological family was kicked

into high gear the second week in November when the

Jespers announced that we would be going to Ohio to

spend Thanksgiving with Mr. Jespers family. I

apologized and explained that I would love to go, but

my grandmother had invited me to spend the holiday

with my own family at her house. Mrs. Jesper was not

receptive to the idea at all, but of course I had

Whalid to back me up. He explained to his parents

that he would not be going to Ohio this year either,

and that he would be spending the holiday with the

Bailleau clan. He assured them that there wouldn't be

any drama, mom and TriAnn had made up and my

grandmother was really set on reunifying me with them.

It was very difficult to get Mrs. Jesper on board with

the idea, but Whalid pleaded with his mom and assured

her that he would be part of my every step and nothing

would happen to me. I think the deciding factor for

her to say yes, is when Whalid told her that my Uncle

Joe lived in the home with my grandmother and he would

definitely be there. She did agree after that was

placed on the table.

In the days following, it was kind of funny but Mr. Jesper was really serious about teaching me self-protection maneuvers. I asked him if he thought I was suppose to use this stuff on my own family members, he stated very clearly, "Lil' Man, anybody who rolls on you wrong has to be taken down, and I don't care what family they belong to!" He made sure I really understood what he was telling me, and I did. He told me I was too small of a guy not to have these tactics on hand, he said, "This is old school stuff, and there's no need for new tricks, all the old ones still work." I got the lessons, though I thought the whole thing was a bit funny.

The next two weeks seemed to be the longest weeks ever, I was so anxious. When the Jespers departed for Ohio on that Tuesday afternoon, I was equipped with numbers to everywhere they would be staying and a list of house rules that I already knew. They also let me know that Whalid would be spending nights in the house with me, since me being there was so new they really didn't want me to be all alone. Whalid suggested it, because he is on vacation from work and he was generally home by himself while my mom is at work in the late hours. His parents were happy he would be there with me, and so was he, but for completely different reasons.

That evening I was wondering where Whalid was, I waited patiently from the time he was off of work for him to show up, before long I was getting a little upset with him, I felt like he was playing me, I ended up going to bed around midnight, all that anger was exhausting. As I lay resting I didn't even hear Whalid let himself into the house around 1am. I was sleeping really good when I felt like I was having a fantastic dream, just about everything on me below the waist was tingling. It felt so real and so good I just continued to slumber and go with it, after awhile it got too involved and I knew I wasn't dreaming and besides I could smell alcohol. I opened my eyes and said, "What are you doing and where the hell have you been?" No answer came, I was just looking down at the top of a head of dreadlocks, he continued to service my body and ignore me. When I knew anything I was being turned onto my stomach, as I felt his hair touching my back and his lips caressing me all over my back, I was drifting into his control as usual, but something in me said, "No, I want answers!" I grabbed a hand full of his hair and stopped him, I said, "Answer me, I been sitting here waiting on you, you didn't even text me or call me." He looked up at me and said, "Oh, now I gotta check in witchu?" I was stunned at how he said it, it was so sarcastic, he had never spoken to me that way. I didn't like it. I rolled to the side of my bed and said, "I beg your pardon, do you have to check in, you don't have to do anything. Just like I don't have to do anything. We have been sneaking and sliding around, maybe I was naïve in thinking I meant something to you, my fault, playa!" He said, "T, don't start that shit, I'm not trying hear all that right now, I'm just trying give you some of this dick and go to sleep." It was clear that he was drunk. That comment infuriated me, I jumped up and stormed to my bedroom door, and said, "Give me some dick and go to sleep! I hope you don't think that you are doing me some favor buddy. Cause I'm not looking for any hand-outs, I'm the one that's been doing you the favor. I'm keeping secrets that you wouldn't want anybody to know and sharing myself with you. So don't you get that fucked up!" He was

looking at me in disbelief, and to be honest I was a
little surprised at myself blowing up at him too. He
jumped up and staggered over to me, he grabbed me by
my arm and said, "Topaz, I'm not trying to argue with
you, you're starting to sound like your mom, she
always fuckin' arguing and shit. I'm not trying to do
all that with both of you. Now can I get some ass or
what, cause you done made me lose my wood with' all
your bitchin', damn!" I pushed him as hard as I
could, which made him stumble onto the bed, he yelled,
"What the fuck T!" I walked over to him and said,
"Don't you ever compare me and my mother like that you
bastard! And who cares about your lost wood, you
must've lost your mind too, cause I'm not having this,
I can't believe you!" I stormed out of the room and
went out into the hallway, I was going to go
downstairs, but before I could make it I was being
dragged down the hallway to his bedroom. He got me
into the room and locked the door behind us. I said,
"Let me out of here Whalid!" He said, "No I'm not,
not until you accept my apology. I didn't mean it,
I'm so sorry, I never want to hurt you, please forgive
me." He had tears streaming down his face, suddenly

all my anger was out of the window. He had fallen
onto his knees with both his arms wrapped around my
legs, I couldn't even move, I said, "OK Whalid, I
accept your apology, please let go of my legs." He
let go and took the lock off the door, I went to leave
out, he said, "Wait a minute, where are you going?" I
said, "To bed, I have to go to school in the morning."
He stood there looking like a child that just dropped
their ice cream cone. He said, "What am I supposed to
do?" I said, "Try starting with taking a shower, then
take your drunk-ass to bed!" I marched down the hall
back to my room, I was pretty proud that I had stood
up for myself. Within 40 minutes I was back in a good
slumber when I felt Whalid's somewhat damp, naked body
pressed up against mine, he was trying to make his way
to get my pajama bottoms off, I turned onto my back
and said, "Excuse me Mr. Jesper, but I believe I made
myself very clear a little while ago." He looked at
me and said, "What," I smiled vindictively and said,
"I still don't want no drunk dick, thanks, but no
thanks." He straddled me in all his nakedness, with
legs across my mid section pinning me to the bed. As
he rested a top of me with himself fully erect in his

hand, he said, "What am I supposed to do with this?"
I looked at him and said, "Well the one thing you did
get right, is you said what are you supposed to do,
cause I'm not doing anything with it, now if you don't
mind, I need to get some sleep." He began working on
himself and said, "Is this it, do you want to see me
make myself pop off? I'll do it if you agree to
finish it, I'll get it started for you. T you are
starting to be off the hook…" I interrupted him, "Boy,
if you don't get outta here with that mess, I'm not
finishing anything – what don't you understand I'm not
doing anything with you, least of all some ridiculous
form of hand to hand combat. Whalid, get on somewhere
and take your drunk ass to sleep." He looked so
disappointed as he rolled over and got under the
blanket and pulled up close to me. I could still feel
the stiffness of his bottom half resting against me,
it was difficult to ignore, but I was determined, he
knew it too. After about 10 minutes he said, "I'm
sorry Baby," I said, "No problem, good night." All at
once I felt his hands sliding around onto the elastic
in the waist of my bottoms, in one sweep he slid them
off, I said, "Damn it, Whalid!" He interrupted my

attack and said, "No T, listen, hear me out." I said,
"Hear what man?" He took his full erect member and
placed it in between my legs a few inches below my
goods and said, "I'm going to leave it here and if you
change your mind, you put it where you want it, ok?"
I said, "Whatever Whalid, you're ridiculous." I layed
there trying to go to sleep for the longest time, it
was such a struggle not to slide down and get it
started, but I held my ground. After about 30
minutes, his erection disappeared and another 10
minutes after that he started snoring. I tried to
catch some sleep for the few hours left before I had
to leave for school; Whalid was sleeping so hard he
didn't even realize I had left in the morning.
Halfway through my day at school I got a text from him
stating that it was going down this evening, so I'd
better be ready. I just smiled, because secretly, I
couldn't wait.

When I got from school, there was no Whalid to be
found. I just did some work around the house and
waited on my payback sex session to get started,
before long, time had gone by, I had gotten tired, and
around 1:30am, I went to bed and thought to myself,

"Here We Go Again!" I had no idea where Whalid was and I was becoming less and less concerned with his whereabouts. This was getting old fast. I layed in that bed but I wasn't sleepy, I was tired and there is a definite difference. I wasn't going to let myself fall asleep, tonight we were going to discuss some things that I wanted straight, I didn't like being placed on hold indefinitely. Whalid finally showed up, I heard him come through the front door, I looked over at the clock, it was 3:17am. By this time I was furious, I got up and walked to my bedroom door and stood in the opening. As I watched him climb the stairs I could see he was drunk again, I just watched in disgust, as he reached the top step. He looked over and said, "Oh, hey Babe, I'm sorry, I should've been here. I met the guys from work for a couple of drinks again, I hope you don't mind." I started to lose the anger and said, "I don't mind you going, but you could've called Whalid, I been sitting here waiting for you, do you know how that makes me feel? It only takes a moment to call or text." He said, "You right T, and I won't do it again. I'm going to go take a shower, and I'm gonna to take care of you,

just gimme a few minutes Luv. All while I was out I
was thinking about coming home and making love to you
for the rest of the night." I stood there and said,
"OK Whalid, and hurry up." Why can't I stay mad at
him, it was driving me crazy, why does he have such a
hold on me?

Once I heard the shower in Whalid's room turn on
I went over into his room and took off all my clothes
and got under the covers and waited on him to come out
of the shower. When he came out and seen me laying
there he said, "Hey Babe, let me finish drying off," I
said, "That won't be necessary, I been waiting all
night, I'm ready for you now, right now." We went at
it for the rest of the night and into the morning, it
was so intense I thought my body was going to give
out. Everytime Whalid would whisper in my ear that he
was so in love with me, I thought I was going to burn
up from the inside out. After we wrapped up our
session we went to sleep in each others' arms, for me
that is one of the best parts. Being in Whalid's
embrace always makes me feel safe and wanted, I loved
it.

We slept until the afternoon, when I woke up I
could hear the alarm going off on Whalid's phone, my
mom had called him quite a few times. I woke him up
and said, "You have messages on your phone Whalid."
He said, "OK Baby, I'm getting up now." He layed
there a few more moments then he finally got up,
grabbed his phone and listened to the messages. He
said, "Oh she is starting already, I don't know how
much longer I can do this, it's starting to wear me
down, man." I said, "Well let me leave so you can
talk," he said, "Hold up T, I need you to do something
for me." I said, "Sure Boo, what's up." He pulled
the covers off of himself and said, "Me, I got wood,
and I need you to knock it down for me." I laughed
and said, "You are so nasty." He told me it was my
fault that these things went on and it was my job to
keep him comfortable. I told him, I was going to need
a raise, because the pay for this job sucked. He
laughed and said, "You can get whatever you want from
the employer as long as you suck too!" It was funny
to me how quickly Whalid could think and comment when
he was talking nasty. I took care of my so-called

duty to Whalid and went to start getting myself ready to get dressed.

Around 3pm we were leaving the house, Whalid had been sitting waiting on me, I took a little longer than normal to get dressed, I was so anxious and I wanted to look good, so everyone knew I was doing ok. I was looking hott, black jeans, black timbs with a black fitted sweater that Mrs. Jesper had custom made for me, it had an area that was attached at the wrists where it fit around your thumb like a glove. I also had a black, across the shoulder, Coach bag. When I came down the steps Whalid looked me over and said, "Damn, we better get goin' before I get to taking all that shit off you, you look good as fuck T. Flat stomach and a bangin' ass and it's all mine." He groped his crotch and smiled like he had just won the lottery. I grabbed my black leather bomber jacket and headed for the door, Whalid said, "We are going to have a ball, you know your gram can cook her ass off. And after you keep making me have sex with you, I'm so hungry." I laughed and said, "Me making you have sex with me, yeah right." We locked up the house and got in Whalid's SUV, as he started it up, I said, "Hey

Whalid, I um…" and I paused. He said, "What Babe?" I said, "I'm a little embarrassed about it," he said, "Embarrassed about what?" I said, "Lately, I been getting…" he said, "Yeah, getting what?" I put my head down and said, "Horny." He laughed and said, "Is that it, that's nothing to be embarrassed about. I'm horny all the time, especially when I think about you." I said, "I know, it drives me crazy, one minute I'm fine and then the next you will come to my mind and then it starts. And…I just had that happen to me." He looked at me with a smile, and said, "Cause you know you love this shit." I said, "I do, and I'm real, real horny right now." Whalid turned the truck off and said, "Oh that ain't no problem, let's go back in the house, we will just be a little late." I said, "No, let's go." He said, "Nah man, c'mon, I'm 'bout to tax dat ass right quick." I laughed and said, "See what I mean, shit-talker. Now who were you saying was sprung over who? I'm not really horny, I was just making a point."

Whalid said, "Well I am now, so let's go in the house." I reached over and kissed him and said, "Later Whalid, I'm hungry." He said, "That's cool, but you're going pay for this later on, I'ma fuck the shit outta you!" I just laughed at him, he's ridiculous.

We pulled up to the front of my grandmother's house and parked, I took a deep breath and said, "OK, so this is it." Whalid said, "Don't worry Boo-Bear I got you." I said, "I know." We got out of the truck and headed toward the house, and there was that empty feeling in my stomach. I told myself there was nothing to worry about. As we reached the porch, the door flew open and out jumped my Uncle Joe, "Wassup nephew!" He grabbed me into his arms and said, "You lookin' good and I hear the Jespers is treating you real good." I said, "Yes Sir, they are. How you been unc'?" He said, "I'm good neph'. You know same ole shit, different day, right." I laughed as he gave Whalid a pound and a hug, and said, "Wassup my nig, you a stand up dude, you kept your word and took care of my baby and I love you for it, I owe you man." Whalid said, "Joe man, that ain't necessary, I'm down for Baby Boy, he's family to me and my folks." We walked into the house, I looked around and I was very happy to see my family members. There were a bunch of them there, cousins, aunts, uncles and all. I hugged

my grandma as she said, "Hello Gene, baby how are you?

I'm so glad you came, we are family and we need to be

together, you hear me? Come with me," she grabbed my

hand and led me to the kitchen where my mom and TriAnn

were sitting at the table. There were a few other

family members in there, Whalid was right behind us.

I said, "Hey y'all, Happy Thanksgiving, I'm so glad to

see y'all!" My mom just looked with an unbothered

expression on her face and said, "Hey." TriAnn

literally rolled her eyes up in her head and walked

out of the kitchen. I could feel my rage beginning to

build, but I told myself, "I'm not doing this today."

I got a soda and started back toward the livingroom

where some of my other cousins were, Whalid followed

behind me and caught me in the hall and said, "You

ok?" I said, "I ain't pressed, I'm good." At that

moment I hear my mom yell Whalid's name. He started

back to the kitchen area, and I heard her tell him,

"Grab a seat, you ain't got to baby that muthafucka!"

My grandmother said, "We ain't doin' this today, we

are gonna repair our family." My mom said, "Whateva!"

As the day went on the shady behavior continued, mom and TriAnn just basically acted like I wasn't there, and whenever we made eye contact they would kind of roll their eyes. It was just pissing me off more and more as the day went on. It was finally time to sit down for dinner and the whole family was gathered in the kitchen area and the dining room area, we all just squeezed in, it used to be a great time for us as a family, but for me now, not so much. I was sitting in my seat across from my mom and next to my grandma for a few minutes and I realized TriAnn and Whalid were both not in their seats next to my mom. I thought it was real cute how they had sat me across the table like I wasn't a part of their family unit. I got up and told my grandma, "I'm going to run to the bathroom real fast." She said, "Hurry up Gene and tell Whalid and TriAnn to get the lead out wherever they are." My mom said, "I don't know where Whalid's dumb ass is, but TriAnn went to the bathroom." I turned my head and looked at her and shot her a dirty look, she looked at me and said, "And… did you have a problem with something I said?" I stared at her and said, "I beg your pardon mom, are you speaking to me?"

She said, "Fuck you and that smart shit, don't get fucked up!" I looked at her and I said, "I think not." She went to jump up and my grandmother said, "Sit your ass down, I ain't having this shit and I am serious Theresa. Gene go on to the bathroom." I was still standing there, I looked at my grandma, and then I proceeded down the hallway. As I was reaching the top of the stairs I could hear whispers, as I got down the hallway I could hear more clearly. I heard Whalid's voice, "You know that's not true, you know that ain't how it went down, don't try to blackmail me, cause I don't play that bullshit. Why are you always so vindictive, and why do you hate her so much?" Then I heard, "Because she's a Bitch and she never did anything for me. And I'm gonna take everything she has that I want, including you." I could tell right away it was TriAnn's voice, I could hardly stand still, I wanted to hurt her. But I stood there so I could make sure I had my info right before I jumped to any conclusion. Whalid said, "No TriAnn you're not going to get me and I'm not being part of all of your bullshit." She said, "You are already a part of it, and you will be mine, period. You can't resist me and you know it, I've already seen that. That dick has my name all over it." Then I heard Whalid say, "Don't fuckin' touch me, you're fucked up!" I shot around the corner; they were standing right in front of the bathroom door, TriAnn had her hand up in Whalid's crotch with a good hold on his business, he was trying to remove her hand as he seen me. I said, "What the fuck ever! This is cute, now isn't it!" Whalid said, "T wait a minute, let me explain…" I interrupted him, "You don't have anything to explain to me, I know this trick and I know how she gets down." TriAnn was standing there with a smug grin on her face, she said, "I'll beat your ass again faggot!" I said, "Trust me, them days are over Boo-Boo, you got me fucked up. What you need to do is stop trying to be Theresa and learn how to be TriAnn. Go get your own man, or get you a good dildo, you fuckin' lonely Bitch!" She tried to lunge at me, to which Whalid grabbed her neck with a death grip; he had her so tightly snatched that she couldn't move. He said, "We are going down to eat and this shit is over, none of us are saying shit, do you fuckin' understand." She said, "Yes, let me go." When he let her go she pushed past us and went back down the hallway toward the steps. He looked at me and said, "T, not a word, I mean it" I said, "Easy Mr. Jesper, don't give me any orders, I'm about tired of all this shit, but you and I will discuss why I didn't know this bullshit was going on later on, do you understand?" He said, "OK Babe, let's just eat and then we'll go." I said, "Maybe we will and then again, maybe not!" We went down stairs and took our seats at the table. My grandmother started talking about having the whole family together and how happy she was. She talked about missing my brother and how much everybody loves me, my sister and my mom. She told us we have a lot to be thankful for. She rubbed my shoulder and said, "Also, I am grateful to Whalid and his parents for helping to keep our family together, y'all are good people, my future son-in-law." I thought, "Son-in-law, was this some more mess that's been discussed and he hasn't said anything. OK now I'm boiling!" But before I could say a word, TriAnn blurts out, "Son-in-law, really Whalid. What's that all about, how you goin' be a son-in-law." I said to myself, "She's getting ready to start up the

TriAnn Show." I interrupted her, "Shut up, for once in your life, just shut up. You are just ridiculous and always trying to get something going!" She stood up and said, "Fuck you faggot, I don't know why you keep coming back, we keep tryna get rid of you. Mom doesn't love you and doesn't want anything to do with you, so why don't you just go away." I stood up and said, "Don't worry, I am going to go away, but not before I let you know how ridiculous this family is. You hate me for no reason and you also hate her for no reason. And mom, I have no idea why you hate me, but the gay thing, that ain't enough, not for all the hate you are displaying towards me. So what is it?" Before my mom could say anything my Uncle Joe had stood up; he said, "I'm sick of this shit, all these muthafuckin' secrets and shit, and that lil' Bitch of yours Threa, you praise her and run behind her and she cuts you every chance she gets. I know what's up and whenever you really want to know Threa, sit down wit' me and I'll let you know, but y'all bitches bet not fuck wit' my muthafuckin' nephew, thats y'all shit. And that's what the fucks up…" My grandmother interrupted, "That's enough Joe; everybody sit down."

TriAnn said, "Fuck your ole loser ass Joe, you can't tell nobody shit about me, you bastard. And you're right, you fuckin' faggot I do hate you, I've told you before you're a Bitch and an embarrassment, you should be like some of the others and go kill yourself, freak ass. But instead you parade around wit girly-ass clothes on tryna be a Bitch. You even got a purse now, what da fuck is that. Then you got people calling you Topaz, I heard about that shit, that ain't your name you gay ass Bitch!" I said, "Actually it is, is it that you're jealous, is that why you can't stand me? What do my clothes and the way I act have to do with you, who could be anymore embarrassing than you two? On the news being hauled out of a church for acting like damn Vikings. I don't do all that; is that the problem? That you're a fat bitch that is upset because you can't wear what I can. Is that why you always want to fight and tear up all my clothes in the process? If you were as dedicated to a diet as you are to hating me, we could be in competition, but right now, there is no competition, is there? Just that one that you and your mammie are in. You want to be your her, so you hate her. And she wants to be young again.

It sounds like an awful Lifetime Movie, you are very sick, and twisted." By this time Whalid had moved from in between my mom and TriAnn and made his way around the table towards me and so had my Uncle Joe. My mom said, "Fuck all this bullshit. I did hear about that renaming yourself shit, it's always something with you and your gay ass, and Joe what the fuck you talkin' bout nigga, you don't know shit." TriAnn interrupted her, "Yes he does, but I'd rather tell you myself. That lil' dude you been sneakin' around with from your job, he likes to sneak around with me too. Joe seen us at the club, but I told you a long time ago you need to get a man your own age, he ain't but 25." Whalid said, "Threa, what the hell?" He grabbed me by my arm and said, "Let's roll!" My mom said, "We're just friends Whalid, but fuck you if you wanna go, then go." She quickly focused her attention on TriAnn, "And what are you trying to do? Are you trying to run behind me with a nigga, you ain't got it like that Bitch." TriAnn said, "How you figure? I fucks dat nigga swell several times a week and every time we're together he sucks my pussy and tells me that he loves me; and I laugh because every time I talk to you, I'm smellin' it on your breath. Cause yeah he told me you sucks his dick and you ain't even good at it, you old ass cougar Bitch!" The family members were holding them apart, you could tell mom really wanted to get to TriAnn. I looked at Whalid's face, he was looking really hurt and betrayed, but he just stood there holding my arm. TriAnn then continued on, "And being as though we're talkin' about my muthafuckin' skills Bitch, why don't we ask Whalid. Ask him who sucks a better dick, me or you Bitch!" The room seemed to start to move in slow motion, and everybody was looking at Whalid. I yanked my arm away from him just as he went into a rage, he said, "Hell no TriAnn, I told you I don't fuckin' play these games, I'm sorry to be disrespectful to this family but y'all ain't going to put me in that shit. Threa, I didn't do shit, I was at the house a few weeks ago and TriAnn let herself in with her key, and got started fucking with me while I was laying on the couch. I was asleep, and when I woke up I pushed her off me and put a stop to it immediately, I didn't say anything because the two of you had just started speaking again and I didn't want to fuck it up, TriAnn tell the truth." TriAnn said, "What truth Baby, you was on a full hard on when I was suckin' his dick, and you know we been makin' plans to finish up, I am gonna let you beat my shit up just like you asked." Whalid interrupted her, "What!!!!! If I was trying kick it with you, why would I be trying to finish up, I would of finished it right then, you're a liar TriAnn. I'm not gonna sit here and be accused of something I didn't do." I wanted to let him hang but I couldn't so I chimed in and said, "It's true, when I was at the bathroom a minute ago, I caught TriAnn trying to set him up and threatening him." TriAnn screamed, "Fuckin' faggot, I'ma fuck you up!" She tried to get at me, but no one would let her, my family contained the situation; they got everybody settled, and I told Whalid, "Get our coats, we are out of here. But not before I give my regards to my family for the last time." I went back to the dining area where some folks were finally eating, my mom was sitting on the far end of the room crying with a few family members huddled around talking to her, my grandma was working

the room trying to keep the peace, and TriAnn was
sitting at the table fussing and cussing. Uncle Joe
was just standing in the center of the room not
amused. I said, "Family I love you, but I can't do
this with you all anymore, Uncle Joe I will love you
'til the day after I leave this planet and beyond.
Grandma thank you for trying, but it's time for me to
move on. There's too much hate and I don't need to
endure anymore of it. Take care of yourself." My mom
yelled out, "I never wanted you, I never wanted you,
get the fuck out!" I said, "It's probably a good
thing that you didn't Theresa Bailleau, because now
you don't have me – You are dead to me! You can rest
in peace, along with your dead son that you wanted."
She tried to get up to charge but to no avail. By
this time Whalid had come back in to see what was
taking so long. TriAnn had jumped up on her feet and
yelled, "Don't say shit about my brother you fuckin
Bitch!" I said very calmly, "I'm going to enjoy
knowing that you are so in denial about why you hate
me so much, and knowing that it is going to eat you
alive from your insides out, you rotten whore. I hope
you and mother get to see your brother, that you love

so much, real soon!" At that point TriAnn grabbed a
hold of my shirt and it was a different ballgame then
she was used to; I wasn't being dragged and beaten up
we were fighting and exchanging blows. She was
tearing my shirt apart and I was tearing hair out of
her head by the handfuls, I'd had enough. We had
overturned furniture and knocked food all over the
floor. My Uncle Joe broke us up single handedly, he
told Whalid to hold me, and he put TriAnn in a chair.
I screamed, "I'm tired of this shit, the next
muthafucka that puts their hands on me is gonna pay
dearly, y'all got me fucked up!" TriAnn said, "I'ma
woop your ass every time I see you faggot, every time,
I promise you that!" I saw my opportunity for revenge
and I seized it, Whalid had let go of me to pick up my
coat and in that split second I made a mad dash while
going into my shoulder bag, I got up to the chair
TriAnn was sitting in before she could brace herself
and I punched her dead square in her mouth with all
the force I could. Me, her and the chair fell over,
my Uncle Joe said, "Whalid get him!" TriAnn was
trying to get up and I was ready, I yelled, "C'mon
Bitch, come and get me, woop my ass like you said you

would! I'm tired of you talking shit. It ends today!" My mom yelled, "Fuckin' faggot," she ran around the table, and I told her, "Theresa Bailleau I don't want to, but I promise you if you run up on me, you will be picking rug lint off of your back!" She kept coming and before she could get to me my Uncle Joe yanked her by her shirt and slammed her to the floor with such force I thought he had broken her neck. He then said, "I fuckin' told y'all, don't touch him!" My grandmother was screaming, "Gene you get out! You done knocked out her tooth, you get out!" I said, "Grandma are you choosing sides?" She just looked at me. I said, "I understand, you always did. You're just a little fake though, I still love you." As I walked out of the door, I looked over my shoulder and I could see the blood running from TriAnn's mouth along with the gaping hole where her two front teeth used to reside.

Once Whalid and I were in his truck I could feel my hand throbbing horribly, I said, "Can you please take me by Emergency?" He pulled off and said, "What's wrong Baby, are you hurt?" I said, "Oh I'm definitely hurt, but it's my hand that I need to be looked at." I had unballed my fist and put my little secret back into my shoulder bag. You see, when I hit TriAnn in the mouth I had a roll of quarters in my hand, I fully intended to knock her teeth out and that's just what I did. I will play the victim no more.

We spent a couple of hours at the Emergency Room, my hand had a very bad sprain, but it was not broken; they wrapped it very tightly in an ACE bandage. We got into the SUV and headed home and I was thinking to myself, "And now, Round Two!" I was still quiet, I was pissed at Whalid and he knew it. We got to the house and I just jumped out of the truck without saying a word, I let myself in and went straight to my room and closed the door. I began to undress and continued on with my anger that was steadily building inside of me. After a few moments I heard a light tap on my door followed by a pitiful voice saying, "Topaz, baby please let me in, please let me explain myself." I opened the door and walked over and sat on my bed, he walked into the room slowly and sat on the bed next to me. He just sat there for a few minutes, so I said, "Don't just sit there, start explaining.

Explain it all to me Whalid; EXPLAIN, how you didn't tell me that you were being blackmailed by my sister. EXPLAIN, how you didn't tell me that my sister had your favorite body part in her mouth. EXPLAIN, how it slipped your mind that you and my mom have been talking about getting married." At that moment, I reached over and hit him upside his head. All of his dreads fell forward into his face, he just sat there, then he said, "I deserved that." I said, "Your damn right you did! Whatever happened to, when you're 18, it's gonna be me and you. Yeah right, how does that work? You, me, my mom and her ring. And who else Whalid who else is there, who else are you fucking, I hate you! I hate your black ass! You used me, you don't love me, you're a liar, a stinking, filthy, vicious fucking liar!" By this time the tears had begun to flow. I dropped my head into my hands. Whalid just flopped back onto the bed, he was covering his face as he started to explain, "I don't want you to hate me, I never lied to you, I never lied Topaz. I knew you wouldn't understand the thing between me and TriAnn, that's why I just kept it away from you, but I was gonna tell you about it after I got it all straightened it out." I sat straight up and interrupted him, "Holding things back from me doesn't work, how many times do I have to tell you that. You love to play the 16 year old card on me, like you're always trying to protect me. Do I really need all that protection, no one was trying to protect me when you took my virginity away, you weren't all worried then. The only worry you had then was if I could get you to a climax. Your full of shit!" He sat up and grabbed me by my arm and said, "Shut your damn mouth, you ain't gonna keep talking to me like that!" I screamed at him, "Take your damn hands off of me, don't start trying to man-handle me fucker. You told the lies, you got your dick sucked, you're the one getting engaged. I'm getting screwed, which is all I've gotten since I been fucking around with you. I was stupid, but no more! I don't want to hear shit else from you!" I slapped his hand off my arm, and got up to finish changing my clothes, I slid my jeans off and threw them into my hamper. Whalid stood up from the bed still trying to explain, "I am telling you, it's not true. I'm not engaged to anybody; I don't know where all that shit came from. I've been

at a point with Threa that I could hardly stand to be
in the room with her without us arguing like cats and
dogs, why would I ask her to marry me? You know deep
inside how I feel about you, I understand you being
mad with all that's gone on today, but you can't just
dismiss me like that." He was standing directly in
front of me at this point, and he was looking down at
me. He said, "T, look at you, how could I not be in
love with you?" I was in nothing but a pair of royal
blue bikini underwear by that time. Whalid reached
down around me and pulled me into him as he spoke, "I
think about you all day, everyday. Even when I'm in
the bed at night with Threa, my mind is over here on
you. You got me fucked up." His hands had slid down,
he was now rubbing my behind, I said, "Is that
supposed to be cute to me? That you are in bed with
my mother and just getting done fucking her, and
you're telling me that you are thinking about me. You
and TriAnn probably would make a good pair, she's all
twisted up too. This sounds like some Lifetime shit.
I'm telling you, I don't like this and I want out!" I
was trying to push Whalid off of me, but he wouldn't
allow it. He had me so tightly wrapped in his grasp

that I couldn't move. He said, "You ain't goin'
nowhere, it's just you and me now, I ain't fucking
with Threa, she fucking cheated on me, I'm done! I'm
gonna get my shit out of that house this week. I'll
be right across the hall, you won't have to be lonely
anymore T, I'll be a few steps away Baby." I said,
"Whalid, are you kidding, I mean, do you hear
yourself? You are mad at her for cheating on you,
what do you think you were doing with me, and sorry
but I think your bullshit was a little worse. You need
to own it and suck it up that she was slicker than you
were, because you didn't catch her, you were clueless.
If you want to move on, then move on, but there is no
need for harsh feelings coming from you, they are not
warranted. But when it comes to me and all of this
mess, this is where I get off the train!" He backed
up from me and pushed his dreads out of his face and
said, "Oh really." I could see clearly what I would
call his angry eyebrows, they were almost meeting in
the middle of his forehead, he leaned forward into my
face and said, "That Bitch wasn't slick, yeah she
tried to play me, but how could she have played me
when I keep my dick in you more than in her. So the

jokes on her, isn't it. And you ain't done with me 'til I say you're done, you belong to me, ain't no other nigga gonna get what's mine. I broke you in with this dick and you're gonna stay on this dick 'til I say I want you off, you got that!" I mugged him in his face with my full hand as hard as I could and started pushing him in his chest, as I was yelling, "Fuck you Whalid, fuck you! You tried to use me for some sick, twisted reason but no more, I'm done with your black ass!" He then grabbed me around my neck and threw me onto the bed and tore my underwear off in one pull, it kind of hurt a bit as the material ripped off of my body. He leaned over and kissed me on my behind and said, "But I'm not done with your ass, not yet, that's my shit! Don't you forget that. I named you and I claimed you!" He stood up as I laid on the bed naked and crying, he gave me a nod of his head and put the torn underwear up to his nose and said, "That's some good ass, it always smells like baby powder and baby lotion. And it's mine, the sooner you figure it out, the better off we will be. And stop crying, you know I don't like it when you cry!" He walked out of my room and slammed the door behind him.

I laid there on the bed for about forty minutes just sobbing; what in the world had I gotten myself into? I still felt safe for some reason with Whalid, I just wasn't sure about his current mind set, I knew he was hurt and angry, and I didn't want him to take out his frustrations on me. I had never had him speak to me that way, it hurt me and made me feel like I was nothing to him. I felt like I was a pawn in some twisted game between him and my mom. After laying there, my worry turned to anger, and I vowed to get back at Whalid, and to turn the table on our interactions. I had three days to work with before the Jespers would be home on Sunday. I plotted and I planned and within the next few hours I was ready to kick it up a notch. I got up and walked my naked body over to Whalid's room, he had dozed off, it was around midnight, I went into his bathroom and took a shower and came out soaking wet. I walked over to the bed and climbed on top of him which woke him up, he just laid still and looked at me and said, "What are you doing, and why is your ass all wet?" I said, "Cause I forgot my towel in my room and when I looked at you I just wanted to get close to you. Is that a problem,

are you still mad?" He said, "A little, I don't like
that smart shit T." I licked his top lip and said, "I
don't really feel like arguing right now, do you have
anything else you'd rather be doing to me right now."
And with that I slid off of him and laid along the top
half of the bed with my legs spread as far apart as I
could. He was looking up at me like a kid in a candy
store. I grabbed him by his hair as he mounted me
with all of his clothes still on, it seemed with in
seconds they were off. He was banging at me so hard
that I could tell he was still upset with me a bit. I
said, "If this is the way you take out your anger, I
just have to piss you off more often. He was really
going at it and grunting and groaning, this was
definitely an anger induced session on both our parts.
He was beginning to verbalize his climax when I threw
my plan into high gear, I told him to let me get on
top, he rolled both of us over and I continued working
him over. As he was starting to tense up I stood
straight up and yanked his condom off with one swift
motion and jumped off of the bed. He said, "What the
hell are you doing T?" I said, "Huh, what do you
mean?" He said, "How you gonna get up and stop before

I skeet?" I looked at him and said, "You need to know, I don't like that smart shit either and further more I don't belong to anyone, I will make love to only who I choose to. And I will make you skeet when I want, not when you want!" And with that I threw the condom on his chest and walked out of the room and slammed the door behind me.

The next day I stayed in my room for most of the day, until I heard Whalid leave out of the front door, he hadn't said anything to me at all. I'm sure he was definitely still mad after that stunt I pulled. I was pretty at ease with Whalid out of the house, the funny thing was as mad as he'd made me I couldn't wait for him to come back. I felt like I must be losing my mind, I know that I am absolutely in love with him and I know this is going to be a dead end, but I can't help it. A few hours went by and as I sat down in the gameroom eating popcorn I heard keys at the front door, I got all excited and had butterflies in my stomach longing to lay my eyes on him. But disappointment followed as I heard him go upstairs and into his room and slammed the door. Could he still be that upset with me, I sure hoped not, I really didn't want him to be mad at me, but I had to keep him in check, he went a bit too far last night. About twenty minutes later I heard him coming down the stairs, but he turned and went into the kitchen. Just as I was convinced that he had written me off, I heard him coming down the stairs to the gameroom, I fought to hold my smile back. He walked into the gameroom and stood over me for a moment, I looked up at him and he immediately leaned over and kissed me and said, "I'm sorry Boo-Bear, I was acting like an ass, do you forgive me?" I said, "I suppose." He reached into my lap and took a hand full of the popcorn that I was eating and started to eat it as he slid close to me on the couch. He said, "What are we watching Luv?" I told him the name of the movie and we sat there and took in a few more movies and just enjoyed each other. We played and wrestled and talked about school and his work, it was perfect. After a few hours I had fallen asleep on Whalid's shoulder. He said, "C'mon, Baby let's go upstairs and go to bed." I said, "OK," I went to get up and he said, "Hold up," and he picked me up and carried me up to the second floor and into his room. Once he locked the door behind us he began to make certain that I knew he was sorry for the previous events, he made love to me the way he did the first day I had given myself to him. The next morning I laid in Whalid's arms just so satisfied, all along knowing that I was right back where I had started, on the outs with my family and all into Whalid.

Now, It's My Turn

It was about 8pm when the Jespers arrived back at the house on Sunday evening, Whalid and I were sitting in the gameroom. When we heard the keys in the door Whalid said, "The honeymoon is over for right now." He kissed me softly on my lips and said, "I'm just across the hall my love, when your body calls, I'm gonna come running to you." I laughed and said, "You are so corny." When actually the silly comment made my insides quiver. We went up the steps to greet them, we all met up in the kitchen, we did our hugs and told them how much we missed them and how glad we were that they were home. We were talking when the room came to a standstill and I heard, "It better not be…" we all looked at Mrs. Jesper. She said, "What is wrong with your hand Topaz?" It was still wrapped in

the ACE bandage from the hospital, I put my hand
behind my back. She said, "Do not hide it, I want
some answers and I want them now!" We started to
explain the events from the Thanksgiving dinner fiasco
at my grandmother's house, as well as the separation
of my mom and Whalid. We never even finished giving
her all the details when she shut us down and said, "I
don't even want to hear anymore, I told you Wade, I
didn't want my baby to go over there with those folks.
It's always an issue. Something in my spirit told me
that this wasn't favorable to send Topaz into. But I
have had enough, I've heard enough and I've seen
enough." She took me into the livingroom where it was
just she and I, I sat down and she said, "I'm sorry, I
just can't take anymore, Topaz. What are your
thoughts on this, because ultimately this is about you
and your relationship with your family, not my
personal feelings." I looked up at her and said, "I'm
ok, Whalid took care of me as much as he could, while
he was keeping himself together; but when it comes to
my family, I'm done! Mrs. Jesper, I don't care if I
never see any of them again, with the exception of my

Uncle Joe." She looked at me with an intense look on her face and said, "Good, because now, it's my turn!"

I had no idea what she meant by that comment, but I knew it would be something very interesting in the upcoming days. In the short time that I've been with the Jespers, I have found that she doesn't play around, and Whalid and his dad kind of stay out of her way when her mind is made up. Shortly after all of that the Jespers said they were tired and they were going to call it a night. Whalid and I decided to watch some more television and around midnight, we also called it a night. It was back to work and school in the morning.

School was pretty uneventful that next day, I was glad, my mind was still spinning with the uncertainty of what was meant by Mrs. Jesper. As a whole, I was enjoying school, it was an entertaining time for the most part, five out of my seven classes had my crew in them. And Mike flirted with me all through the day, what can I say it was an ego builder. Sometimes it even made me a little nervous, because I would find myself saying, "I wonder how he is?" But the urge

would generally pass with the thought of my dread-
headed Adonis that I had at home.

When I jumped off of the school bus and started
up the walkway to the house I could smell fantastic
fragrances. I sped up my steps, let myself in and
went straight to the kitchen where I found Mrs. Jesper
in her apron and cooking up a storm. I said, "Good
afternoon, what's going on, it smells wonderful in
here." She said, "Baby, I'm feeling good today, I
took off work this day, because today is an important
day, it is a life changing day and it's a day for
family. That is all I'm going to say for now. I want
you to get dressed for a proper dinner and be down
here at 6pm, so get all your homework and everything
done, ok Baby." I said, "Yes Ma'am, I'm going now."
She said, "That's my Baby!"

I was hurrying to get all my work done so I could
be downstairs and ready on time, I was just dieing to
see Mrs. Jesper had going on. I ran in Whalid's room
to get my toothbrush out of his bathroom; though I had
full access to the bathroom in the hallway, I always
found myself in his, go figure. The Jespers had four
bathrooms in all, one attached to their room, the one

in Whalid's room, mine in the hallway a few steps from my bedroom and one on the main floor of the home. Anyway, as I went into Whalid's bathroom he was in the shower, I went over to the sink to grab my toothbrush and I couldn't help looking at his image behind the sliding glass shower doors, he was just so damn sexy. He was looking back at me, he slid the door open and said, "I was thinking about you before you even came in here." I said, "Oh really," he slid the door all the way open to show me the proof. I said, "Boy, I ain't got no time to fool with you right now, I can't wait to see what your mom's got up her sleeve." He said, "I don't have a clue. But don't worry." He reached down and began touching himself and said, "You got a minute for a nigga that loves you?" I laughed and said, "No, not at this moment, but I love you back." He said, "No worries, I'll take care of this, but later on I'm gonna need to see you," he was steadily working on himself. Then he looked down in his hand and said, "He needs to make a connection with you." I said, "I don't mind hooking up with him later either." I left him to himself and finished getting myself together.

We were all seated at exactly 6pm wondering what we were in for, though I had a feeling that Mr. Jesper knew, because he seemed a bit more upbeat than normal. We were all dressed like we were going out for dinner, the table was set with all the Thanksgiving fixings that you could think of, there was turkey and stuffing, greens, string beans, macaroni and cheese, yams, mashed potatoes, potato salad, ham and cranberry sauce. And just when you thought it couldn't get any better, on the countertop was a peach and apple cobbler and a homemade pound cake. Mrs. Jesper said, "I want to start by asking Wade to lead us in prayer, I'm very happy to be here with all my family to celebrate a good ole fashioned Jesper Thanksgiving dinner. There is no way I would let the holiday go by knowing that you two didn't even get to eat, that really hurt me. So, we are going to be thankful for one another and eat good tonight. So come on Wade, baby, open us up in prayer." We all joined hands as Mr. Jesper lead the prayer, and then all the eating began. As we took in our meal, Mrs. Jesper dropped a bomb on us. She stated, "Topaz, my sweet new edition to this household, I know I kind of confused you last night with our little talk, so allow me to clarify.

You are not a roomer here in this home, you are not

some squatter taking up a room, we see you as a part

of the family. We love you as much as we love Whalid.

Wade am I right?" Mr. Jesper said, "You know I've

told you that I love you Son, just as you are, and I'm

really glad you are with us!" Mrs. Jesper continued,

"Whalid, it's time to end this charade, you need to

remove your things from Theresa's house, you said you

are done with that situation, be done, come on home,

and then you can figure out your next move, but the

separation needs to happen." Whalid said, "I agree

Mama, I already had that plan, this evening when

Theresa goes to work I'm going to move my stuff, I

don't want any issues with her, I wish her the best, I

just don't want her as part of my life anymore." Mrs.

Jesper continued, "Topaz, the last thing I said to you

is, it's my turn. And it is, it is time for me to

handle things the way I handle things. I've been to

see our lawyer, and I have begun the ball to rolling,

you are a part of this family, and so you shall be.

Wade and I will be fighting for legal custody of you."

She paused and waited for a response, I was in shock I

didn't know what to say, Whalid's mouth just dropped

open. She continued, "It makes no sense to allow this

foolishness to go on any further, the best years of

your life are upon you and you need family in your

corner not all this craziness. I will seek for

support payments from Theresa and we will set it up in

an account for you. Now that's me being a little bit

vindictive, we can afford to raise you, but why should

she get a free ride, she owes you that support and we

will see that you get it. She hasn't been in your

corner mentally, but she will financially, period. So

there you go, that is my plans, but if you do not

agree, I can stop the proceedings immediately." I

said, "No, I am ecstatic, that you all love me that

much, that you would…" I couldn't go any further, the

tears started coming. Whalid got up and walked over

to me, he knelt down beside my chair and said, "It's

going to be ok T." We finished dinner and cleaned up

the dishes and put the food away, I was so full I just

needed to lie down. The last thing I heard Mrs.

Jesper say to Whalid was not to have me out all night

moving those clothes and things because I have school

tomorrow. I hate moving and carrying stuff around,

but that's my dude, so I'm all in. I had a good sleep

going when Whalid woke me up and said it was time to

go, it was a little after 1am. We went over to the

dark lifeless house and began packing up all of

Whalid's and my belongings, by 2:30am we had

everything at the front door ready to be loaded into

his truck. Whalid said, "Did you get everything you

wanted from your room," I said, "Yes," Whalid pulled

me up close to him and said, "How bout we get even."

I said, "Get even, what do you mean?" In that moment

he swept me up and carried me upstairs to my mom's

room and made love to me all over her room, I don't

think there was a piece of furniture in that room that

I didn't lean over, bend over, sit on or lay on.

Though it was mean to do, I felt so empowered by our

shady act. We walked back down the steps and loaded

all of our things into Whalid's SUV. As we were about

to lock the house up, I said, "Can you go one more

time?" Whalid said, "You know my shit's always on

brick!" I led him to the diningroom and crawled up

onto the center of the table and let Whalid have his

way with me right there in the middle of the

diningroom table. As Whalid did his business I said

to him in his ear, "I win, I got the man, and a real family. Now, it's my turn!"

<u>Now The Real Fighting Starts</u>

"You fuckin' bastard, I'm glad you left and took all your shit. Cause Stan moved in today and I'm glad I don't have to sneak to get me some good dick anymore, you fuckin' loser." This was the message that was left on Whalid's phone by mom. It had been three days since we had moved our things out of the house, and she had already moved in the guy that she and TriAnn were both messing around with. I couldn't believe that she would continue on with him knowing that he was having sex with my sister. I couldn't understand that. It was surprising that she didn't lash out at Whalid on the first day that she noticed he was gone, but I guess she had other plans on getting rid of him anyway. Whatever, he and I were very happy being so close to each other, and there was nothing like having access to my dude almost whenever I wanted. So I guess I should've thanked mom for being ridiculous. She didn't bother with me at all, she hadn't said a word about my things being removed, I guess she didn't care, that's so typical.

About two weeks after that we received letters stating the request for custody and a subpoena to appear in court on January 9th, which just happens to be my birthday. This was going to be such a great

birthday present for me, the best ever. I really want

the separation and I want to be done, really done.

One week after we got the letter, Mrs. Jesper and I

were out doing our normal, shopping on a Saturday. We

had decided to stop and grab a few groceries before we

headed back to the house. We were going up and down

the aisles, I was enjoying every minute of it, Mrs.

Jesper was like a good-good girlfriend and a mom all

wrapped into one. I rarely asked her for anything,

yet she was constantly buying me things. I would try

to pay for lunch or things sometimes and she wouldn't

have any part of it. I had a pretty good nest egg

saved, Whalid was constantly giving me money. He said

I was his and he wanted me to have no reason to ask

anyone for anything.

Out of the corner of my eye I thought I had seen

TriAnn but wasn't quite sure. We kept it moving, as

we made another turn into the frozen food section

standing directly in front of us was mom. She

immediately started going in, she approached us and

said, "So you want my faggot do you, do you think I

care, because I don't. I never wanted him from the

time I found out I was pregnant." Mrs. Jesper
interrupted her, "Listen Theresa, we have never had
this kind of dialogue between us and we are not going
to start this, especially not in public." My mom
continued to snap, "You can't tell me what kind of
dialogue that I'm gonna have when it comes to
something I shit outta my ass. You're not my mother,
and your punk ass son is not here." I could see Mrs.
Jesper was getting irritated, she said, "Let me tell
you something, little girl, you need to get yourself
together. All of this unnecessary venom you're
spitting is not helping anyone, and I will not
continue to listen, your days of verbally abusing both
of my sons is over. Now take your little cart and
your bad attitude and get on!" It was starting to get
a little loud and folks were starting to stare. My
mom then really went in and said, "Your son, he is not
your fuckin' son you sidditty-ass suburb bitch. I
will never let you have him, I don't want the
cocksucker but you're not getting him!" I said, "Why
don't you stop it, why don't you just let me go!" By
this time TriAnn had come around the bend into the
aisle, she threw her purse in mom's cart and ran up in

my face and said, "Didn't I tell you I was gonna fuck

you up every time I see you Bitch!" Mrs. Jesper

stepped in front of me and said, "I swear to the

almighty if either one of you put your hands on him,

the undertaker will dress you for a fantastic party

this weekend!" TriAnn started mouthing off to Mrs.

Jesper, "Why do you want to protect him anyway, what

is your point, the world hates fags like him. He's a

filthy faggot-ass muthafucka." I said, "And you are

jealous, jealous because you know the world doesn't

hate me, it burns you up, both of you, that I look

like her and I'm small like her and you look like a

linebacker, you big hairy back Bitch! And guess what,

I hate the both of you!" Mrs. Jesper grabbed my hand

and said, "Baby, you don't stoop to meet these

mongrels in the playground, you let them play alone!"

My mom pulled TriAnn back and told Mrs. Jesper, "I

will slap the shit outta you if you say another word,

you old Bitch!" Mrs. Jesper replied, "I've heard

enough, let's go Topaz." We started moving toward the

front of the store, they were following behind us with

a steadily growing crowd, TriAnn said, "I'm gonna get

him, I swear I'm fuckin' him up. I owe you, you

Bitch!" The in-store security broke up the crowd, the
security guard came directly up to Mrs. Jesper and
said, "Trudy what's going on, and how can I help."
She said, "These lovely people are bothering me and my
child, please send them away Earl." Without a second
to spare, mom and TriAnn were being escorted out into
the parking lot.

We finished checking out and Mrs. Jesper thanked
her friend that was working security, then she told
me, "You see Baby, sometimes you can get around
ignorance. Now don't get me wrong, sometimes you have
to get down and dirty, but at the end of the day, she
is your mother and I want to be respectful to her in
your presence. But that is the last time that I will
excuse her being in my face speaking about either one
of my children, I just won't have it." I told her,
"Don't worry about me, I wanted to knock them out."
Mrs. Jesper replied, "No matter what she is still your
mother, and parents are to be respected, it is in
God's word." We got out to the parking lot and as we
started across the lot to our car, TriAnn and mom ran
up to us arguing again. Mrs. Jesper said, "Go away,
you have your day in court to say whatever is on your

mind." Mom was yelling, "Calling my son Topaz, his name is Eugene, he ain't no girl. You got that bitch!" Mrs. Jesper said, "If he followed your lead he wouldn't know what his name was, he'd be thinking his name was faggot and bitch. I'm going to tell you one more time, go away Theresa, you are starting to upset me, ok, so run on now little girl." Mom blurted out, "Little girl; you fuckin' old ass bitch!" Mrs. Jesper said, "OK, that's it, I'm done. Topaz, get in the car." I was just about done putting the bags into the trunk when TriAnn came around to the side of the car and started up again, I told her to get out of my face. She continued on, "Topaz, where the fuck did you get that bullshit from, you really want to be a female, you faggot-ass bitch!" I said, "You know what TriAnn, I'm really not a bitch, I just play one in your life!" She swung at my face and missed, I immediately grabbed the crowbar from the trunk and began pounding her with it, she was trying to move out of the way of the beating, but I was on her like a cheap coat and continued punishing her with it. She lost her footing and fell to the ground over on the side of the car where my mom and Mrs. Jesper were, I was so upset, I just kept banging her with the crowbar. Mrs. Jesper was yelling for me to stop. My mom ran over and punched me in the side of the head and said, "You fuckin' faggot!" Mrs. Jesper grabbed mom by her hair and slammed her into a nearby car and said, "I warned you about this didn't I, I'm not playing games here Theresa." Security was approaching quickly, as mom spit directly into Mrs. Jespers' face and said, "Fuck you Bitch!" Mrs. Jesper hauled off and punched my mom dead square in the nose, which knocked her out. The security took us back into the store to write up a report of the incident, once my mom came to, she and TriAnn were sent away.

Later on that evening I was just laying on my bed and had dosed off for a little bit when I felt someone touching my stomach. I awoke to Whalid's smile. He said he was pissed off about the fight and all the drama, but he said he had also heard that I was quite handy with a crowbar. I told him I was tired of all of it, and he said not to worry. Then he dropped some news on me. He would be moving out in the weeks to come, I immediately thought it was another woman and he would be shacking up with her, while I'll be left

here alone with his parents. I was not amused, but he
assured me that there was no one else and it was his
own apartment. Also he informed me of all the time
that I would be spending there. I smiled as he
climbed up onto my bed with me and started kissing me.
Then he asked me if I felt like swingin' on some more
crowbar. I got up and made sure the door was locked
and once it was secure, I went back to the bed,
climbed into his lap and he took it from there. These
stolen moments with Whalid always sent me to a place
where I could just forget about all the confusion and
I can be peaceful and calm.

As the holiday season moved on, I was having the
time of my life, it was one of the best that I could
ever remember having. Yet, my dreaded other half was
really catching a hard time, my mom was constantly
sending him rude texts and calling his phone late at
night while she was on breaks at work and just cursing
him out and blaming the whole situation on him. I
told him to change his phone number, but he wouldn't,
he said he wouldn't let her run his life. I would've
just changed my number, I would rather not speak with
her at all. But it does drive me crazy when we are

stealing some time and here she is butting in with her foolishness. A couple of times I tried to snatch the phone out of his hands but he just wasn't having that, I thought it was pretty funny.

One week before Christmas Whalid informed me that he had found an apartment about twenty minutes away from the house, I don't know how I really felt about that. I didn't know if that was good or bad, what would this do to the dynamic of our relationship? I figured I would just have to wait and see. On the 23rd the Jespers hosted an elaborate holiday party at the house, it was really top of the line. Mr. Jesper and Whalid wore black tuxedos, Mrs. Jesper and I had our outfits custom made. She wore a beautiful red silk strapless gown and I had a red and black tux, the jacket was done in an intricate brocade, we all looked fabulous. At the party there were a few of our neighbors and a good bit of folks from the church that the Jespers attend. I've been to the church a few times, but I'm not made to go if I don't feel like it. All night long I have been getting the strangest looks from Trent. He is the choir director at the church, I noticed him a few times at church, he is really cute, tall and has an undeniable chocolate complexion. His

voice is really deep, especially when he sings, it's

really good quality. As the night went on we decided

to sing Christmas carols, I was happy to do so,

because I was feeling a little bummed out after Whalid

left, he had to attend his job's Christmas party too.

We were singing Silent Night and I kind of zoned out,

I hadn't even noticed that everyone else had stopped

singing. I had my eyes closed thinking of Whalid and

singing and went I opened my eyes everyone was just

standing there staring at me, I was looking around at

them, then I said, "I'm sorry, was I off or was I too

loud?" Mrs. Jesper walked over to me slowly and said,

"Topaz, you never told us you could sing, my God, what

a gift he has laid upon your shoulders." By this time

Mr. Jesper was standing on the opposite side of me,

with his chest poked out as far as any proud father

that you've ever seen. The guests were snapping

pictures of the three of us and clapping, I was

getting a little embarrassed, I could feel my cheeks

heating up. I said, "Thanks guys, it's just something

I don't do often, but I like it." At that point,

Trent introduced himself again, he said, "I know

you've seen me at the church and you've been more than gracious tonight. My name is Trent Dobson and I am the choir director of Mt. Temple Church. I would love to sit with you and talk to you about your singing, and see if you would be a good fit for our choir. Only if you want to, but what I just heard from you young man was heaven sent." Mrs. Jesper stepped in, she said, "OK Trent, we will talk it over with Topaz and we will be in touch with you soon." He said, "Thank you very much Sister Trudy." The carols continued after that for about another forty minutes and then the party was starting to draw to a close. I was in the study retrieving the coats of a few guests as they requested them, when I turned to go back out, and in walks Trent. He walked straight up to me and said, "I just want to say, you have the voice and the face of an absolute angel." He was staring down at me with a great intensity, I just tried to keep my cool as I looked up at his well suited 6 foot 3 inch frame and beautiful white teeth. I said, "Thank you so much Mr. Dobson." He said, "No, No Topaz, I'm only 24, you can call me Trent, I'm sure you and I will be able to make beautiful music together." He then leaned over a kissed me softly on my lips, my feet were stuck in that spot. He pulled away slowly and I put my hand up to my mouth, he said, "I hope I wasn't too out of line but I couldn't help myself." I replied softly, "No, that's ok!" He stepped in closer to me and placed his hand around my waist and planted a few soft pecks on my neck and said, "Damn, you taste just like something straight out of a bakery, so sweet, so sweet." I placed my hand up to his chest, he looked into my eyes deeply and said, "Merry Christmas, Songbird." He planted one more soft kiss against my neck and strolled out of the study. I was in a state of shock, I just couldn't wrap my head around how easily I allowed Trent to swoon me. I love Whalid to death, yet I did nothing to stop Trent's advances, and quite frankly they left me a bit horny. After cleaning up a bit, me and the Jespers turned in for the night, I was in a deep slumber when I visualized myself and Trent getting down and dirty. It felt so real that I could hardly tell that it wasn't really going on, every touch was sending chills through my body. I was rolled onto my stomach and all my clothes were off, I was so aroused and taken back by this dream, but I didn't get a burst of reality until I felt locks of hair touching my back. It startled me and awakened me, I immediately started to feel guilty. I tried to move, but the weight of Whalid's body on top of me kept me still. I said, "Let me up Whalid," he said, "Wassup, I was just gettin' ready to run up in, please don't make me stop." I said, "I just can't right now." He said, "Did I do something, or did I hurt you?" I replied, "No, I just need a couple of minutes." I sat on the edge of the bed and tried to gather my thoughts. Whalid slid over next to me and said, "What is it, are you ok T?" I replied, "Yes, but have I told you lately that I love you." He looked at me funny and said, "You always do, what's goin' on." I laughed and played it off. I said, "You are always coming in here when I'm sleep and taking advantage of me, you nasty night-crawling freak." He laughed and said, "Man, I get so excited to get up in that sometimes I just forget to wake you up. I tell you all the time how good it is, that's real talk Boo. It ain't like nothin' else I ever had." I jumped in, "Speaking of that, what else have you had Whalid? You never really talk about your past with me, so let's talk." He tried to lay me down while saying, "I don't wanna talk about no old in the past shit, I wanna make you feel good right now." I said, "What would make me feel good is some answers and you're getting nothing 'til I get them." He sat up and said, "Dag, I'll tell you," he went onto explain, "I've only had three girlfriends counting your mom, and I've only had sex with a total of five people, and that's including you. I was a virgin 'til I was 15 and me and my first girlfriend had sex, we were both 15, we really didn't know what we were doing. Then when I turned 16, I had sex with a 22 year old girl that used to live about two streets over." I interrupted, "How'd that come about, she was six years older." He gave me a funny look and said, "She told me that she kept seeing me playing ball and could see that I was working with something, cause it was always flopping in my shorts." He was sitting there with a dumb ass grin on his face, I punched him in the chest and said, "Go on clown," he said, "You know wassup," as he held onto himself. He continued, "that went on for about two years until she got engaged and eventually got married, then she moved away. About a month after that the chick who was her maid of honor rolled up on me and told me that ole

girl had told her I was holdin' 11 and she didn't

believe it. I told her if I showed her she'd have to

suck it and she said absolutely, and she did just

that. We dated for awhile, but it didn't work out,

for her to be 24, she was really immature. I took a

break for awhile and then I ended up meeting your mom,

and I really liked her. And you know the rest." I

punched him again and said, "how are you gonna just

lump me in to the rest. You punk!" He said, "You

know how I feel about you, Baby you the best. Now, I

answered the questions. Can I please have my

dessert?" I peeled off his clothes and took care of

him and he most graciously took care of me like he

always did. We laid and talked for awhile before he

tip-toed back across the hallway to his room.

Christmas Day was the absolute best, it was like

nothing I had experienced, I don't even know when the

Jespers had bought all of the gifts they had for me,

and Whalid was no slouch. It was just ridiculous, the

amount of shoes, boots and clothing I received from my

new family. I kept crying all day long, I was just so

happy, and I was really overwhelmed when I gave my

gifts to each of the Jespers, as they didn't even

expect a gift. I had all three of them sit on the

couch and I handed them each a box which made me start

crying all over again. I gave each of them a gold

necklace with a small topaz charm dangling from it.

As they opened their boxes I made them promise that

they would never forget me. Mr. Jesper started with

the tears and before long we were all breaking down,

it was the most beautiful Christmas ever. Late in the

evening on Christmas, Whalid came to my room and said

he had to speak to me. I sat on the bed and asked him

what was up, he told me he had another gift for me but

I had to promise that I would be his from here on out.

I said, "I thought that was the understanding all

along," he said, "I'm just making sure." He kissed me

softly on my lips and said, "I am so fucked up about

you, sometimes I think I'm goin' crazy. I love the

shit outta you T. You gotta be mines for always," and

with that he slid a small box in my hand. I opened it

and there it was, a 2 karat band of topaz; it was

absolutely the most gorgeous ring I have ever seen. I

felt like I was going to faint, I jumped up off the

bed and into Whalid's arms. He was holding me up in

the air and kissing me, then he said, "I take it, you like it." I said, "Are you serious it is beautiful!" He put me down and grabbed my hand and kissed the ring on my finger and said, "I love you so much, Merry Christmas to you Baby-Boo!"

For the next few days I was walking around like I was in a daze, how could anything get any better than this, could this really be my life. Whalid had moved into his new place and I was there just about all of the time, I could definitely get used to this. Mrs. Jesper was always telling me how much Whalid loves me, she said he always wanted a sibling and she couldn't have more children. When she seen my ring the day after Christmas she pulled me into the kitchen and told me, "See I told you, your brother loves you, I almost died keeping that secret from you, I knew you would love that ring, it took us a month to find it." I was floored, because I didn't know what we were going to tell her about the ring being as though, he didn't give it to me during our family gift exchange, but he had explained to his mom that he didn't want the ring to over shine all of the other great gifts that had been purchased. And with that explanation

she never even caught on. Oh well, it was a little
white lie that was definitely for the best. He loves
me and that is what was important.

January 9th seemed to arrive faster than ever
before, as I arose from the bed that morning I felt
like I was carrying a huge weight. There was so much
that was going to go on that day and I didn't know if
I was ready. It was my birthday and also my custody
hearing, I hadn't seen my mother since the fiasco in
the grocery store. Would she still be yelling and
screaming, or would she just not show up and just let
the Jespers have custody without a fight? Who knows?

But my day got better almost instantaneously, I
came down stairs dressed in all black leather, riding
boots, pants and button down shirt, custom-made of
course, it was a gift from Mrs. Jesper. I made my way
to the kitchen for breakfast, and of course I was the
last one to make it, Whalid and Mr. Jesper were
already eating, they started laughing like little kids
when I sat down. Mr. Jesper said, "Sorry Lil' Man, we
couldn't wait, you know you're slow when you get
dressed." Then stood up and said, "I got you a gift
for your 17th birthday, that I know you are gonna love.

Bring it in Trudy!" Mrs. Jesper came in from the
livingroom with a black mink, hooded bomber jacket. I
just fell back in my chair, it was the most gorgeous
coat I've ever seen in person, I looked over at Mr.
Jesper and just busted out crying. He said, "Now, now
Lil Man, don't do that, you know I don't like to see
you cry." And for one second it was like I was in the
twilight zone, because when he said it, he sound just
like Whalid. I got up and ran over and hugged him and
said, "Thank you so much, I love it!" Whalid said,
"The gift giving is not over! Give me your ring." I
gave him a strange look and I hesitated, he said,
"Trust me T, give it here, and close your eyes." So I
did it, and I could feel him trying to slide my ring
back on, and when he eventually he got it on, it felt
a little funny. Then he said, "OK now look," I fell
back in the chair again, as I could hardly catch my
breath looking down at my finger. Whalid had
purchased a 2 karat diamond wrap band, that encased my
topaz ring in the center. My finger was so totally
blinged out, I couldn't stop looking at it. I gave
him a hug and said, "Wow, I really love it, thanks you
guys, this is already turning out to be the best

birthday I've ever had." I sat and tried to eat but I didn't get much down before we had to get headed to the lawyer's office, he was going to brief us on today's proceedings.

It was a little overwhelming to hear what was going to transpire at the hearing, the questions that were going to be asked, the evidence that will be presented and all the extras for "just in case." The lawyer, John C. Foxworth III was a well respected criminal attorney who was doing a favor for a friend, he didn't usually deal with cases as small as ours, but the Jespers are very well connected and have a lot of friends that they have kept through their college and their earlier years of being in the workforce. Mr. Foxworth ensured me that everything would be fine and I didn't have to worry, and that he would complete our family without a problem. He explained that the Jespers really wanted to seek full adoption but if they do that my mom would not be responsible to pay support, so what we would be going after is legal custody and guardianship. He made sure that I completely understood and was in agreement with everything. As we were discussing the situation,

Whalid stated to Mr. Foxworth if in some strange event that his parents can't get custody, that he would be willing to try. Mr. Foxworth said, "Thanks young man, but I think we'll be fine on today's proceedings," he looked over at me and said, "Young man I hope you know how fortunate you are to have a family love you so much, these situations are few. Generally a child your age will end up in foster homes or stuck with family members that abuse them. I am very happy for you, and Happy Birthday to you son." I said, "Thank you." Mr. Jesper said, "Topaz we have one last surprise for you and you will have to agree and sign off on it." I was totally confused at this point. Mr. Foxworth went into his drawer and pulled out a black folder and laid it open on his desk in front of me and he began, "In the event that we are granted custody, the Jespers have explained to me how much they want you to feel complete and whole, they would like you to share their last name." I began to cry, but I managed to force out the words, "Of course, my Gosh, thank you…Are you sure?" I was looking at all of the Jespers, all three of them were smiling and shaking their head yes. Mr. Foxworth continued, "OK, so you would need to sign here at the bottom and print your original name underneath, but before you do that, Mrs. Jesper did you want to say something before we finish this?" She said, "Definitely, thank you John. Topaz do you remember the conversation we had when you gave me permission to call you Topaz instead of Eugene, you told me that you did not like that name, so I like the name Topaz Jesper, what do you think?" I got up and ran over to Mrs. Jesper and hugged her, I said, "Is that possible, can I have that, will the courts let me have it?" Mr. Foxworth said, "You should have a new name to go along with your new life, leave all the rest of the hurt behind, and Topaz, don't ever look back!" I signed the papers and they finally got me calmed down so that we could proceed to the hearing.

We were the first to arrive, we had taken our seats and shortly after that my family members started to arrive, they all seemed to have an attitude, which I expected. There was my mom, my grandma, TriAnn and my Uncle Joe. My Uncle Joe walked over and hugged me and shook hands with the Jespers and said, "I thank you for all that you've done, please take good care of my nephew, and if you need anything please don't hesitate to call me." He wrote down his cell phone number and then went back over and took his seat with my family. My mom and grandma said something to him, I couldn't hear what, but I could see on his face that it wasn't anything nice. Once the trial began it was so quiet and serious inside of the courtroom. They called Mrs. Jesper to the stand, the judge asked her to identify herself, then asked why she was there, Mrs. Jesper began, "My son began dating Ms. Theresa Bailleau almost two years ago, I had some concerns because there was a significant age difference and she also had three children already, but everything seemed to be ok, then almost a year in, Whalid moved in with the family. At that point he started to consult with me about the youngest of the three children, he told me the child was going down the road of being homosexual and the rest of the family wasn't taking it very well and that they could be downright abusive to this child. Whalid started to bring Eugene around us with him periodically and I could see that this child was in need of love, he seemed to be bonding with Whalid, but the more I heard

and seen the interactions of the other people in that
home it bothered me. Everything escalated in July of
last year when I witnessed some physical abuse coming
from the sister and the mother just let it go on. My
husband and I took Eugene home that evening and he
stayed overnight, about three days after that Whalid
brought him back to our house after a physical
altercation with the mother and the sister, but this
time somewhat apparently stomped him in his back and
he now had 6 or 7 stitches in his back. A day later
at a funeral for one of the other Bailleau children, I
witnessed the mother and sister attacking Eugene
again, there was an arrest of these two women when
they began fighting and ultimately disrupted that
whole home-going celebration. My husband and I took
Eugene home with us and that is where he has been ever
since. There was one attempt for reunification during
the Thanksgiving holiday, which also resulted in a
fight and a bad hand injury suffered by Eugene. I
couldn't stand it anymore, and that is why I am
seeking legal guardianship of Eugene Bailleau. Once
the papers were filed and distributed, Eugene and I
were attacked in a grocery store by Theresa and

TriAnn, and I do have statements from the store's security crew." The judge told Mrs. Jesper she could go back and take her seat.

Next to the stand was my mother, the judge asked her what her reaction was to the allegations, she began, "Families have problems sometime but we always work through what our issues are. Now there have been times when it has gotten physical and I am not proud of that. I love my children, all three of them, and it just broke my heart when I received the letter saying that the Jespers were trying to take my baby away. And all of this came after I broke off a relationship with their son, I believe this is his way of getting back at me!" She had the nerve to begin to cry, then she went on, "I don't have any issue with Gene's homosexuality, at first it was a little hard for me but I am in a good place personally. Now, where I do have some concerns is with the change in his personality. Your honor my Eugene was soft spoken and very mannerable, now he is cursing and on Thanksgiving he literally knocked his sister's two front teeth out, then he beat her in the back with a crowbar on another occasion. And he even went as far as to threaten to do bodily harm to me. I don't like this hostile behavior, it has to be coming from their home, he never showed signs of this when he was with me. We've been trying to get Gene to come home, we want him with us, where he belongs, with his family." The judge asked, "Are you telling me that you have been working to reunite with Eugene Bailleau?" She said, "Yes sir, whenever I can get his attention, he is not always open to speak to me. I believe that the Jespers are trying to poison my son's mind against me. I can't stand it, please come home Eugene, mommy loves you!!!!!" She broke down in tears, it was a fabulous performance worthy of an Oscar. The judge said, "I have no other questions please go and take your seat." I looked at Mrs. Jesper and I said, "She is lying, she is lying, oh my God, they are gonna make me go back to her, please don't let them, please." The tears began to run. Mrs. Jesper said, "Stop crying Baby, you aren't going anywhere just tell the truth and remember God knows truth and he upholds it, ok, we can't lose, we've got God on our side." She kissed me on my forehead and moments later I was called to take the stand. The judge asked me basic questions about my home life with my mother and I replied, "It wasn't always terrible, though I always knew that she had issues with my sexuality. She would make comments about how I walk, she would say that I switch more than my sister and that's foul. Then she hated my clothing choices, any clothing that had a tight fit she refused to buy and I would have to get it on my own however I could, then once I did, she would criticize me for having it on the whole time I was wearing it. Within the last year or so, really a few months before Whalid moved in with us, her comments got to be worse. She and my sister would call me the B-word and also refer to me as a fag, or a C-sucker." You could hear a pin drop in the courtroom. "Once Whalid came, he wouldn't speak that way to me, and she would attack him for it. She would tell him that he didn't have to be nice to me, and sometimes it seemed that she got mad because he was. But he never did any of that, instead he would take me places with him, a lot of times we would go to his parents' house for lunch and stuff. Or just play video games over there, he said he could tell when I needed a little break from the criticism. Now that I am at the Jespers' home all the time, I feel complete, I feel loved. No

one judges me, all they ever do is make sure I have

what I need. Now I definitely have chores and rules

that I have to follow, but no ones yelling and

screaming and most importantly your honor…" I got a

little chocked up and started to cry a bit as I

continued, "they don't hit on me, or throw food or

drinks on me." The judge just stared at me for a

moment, I could tell in his eyes he knew I was telling

the truth. He said, "Thank you young man, you can go

back and take your seat." The judge asked if there

was anyone else that wanted to share any testimony, to

which my grandmother raised her hand. He motioned for

her to come up and be sworn in, and she began, "Your

honor, I just wanted to say, that as a grandmother it

saddens me when someone would so selfishly try to tear

a family apart. We welcomed Whalid and his family in

so graciously and now for them to be trying to rip my

daughter's child away from her when she just suffered

the loss of another child is just the devil's work.

Then they don't call him by his birth given name, they

call him some ole name that little gay friends of his

use to refer to him. It's just wrong, why they would

promote that kind of lifestyle onto my grandchild, it just sickens me." The judge sat up really straight and said, "Ma'am would you like to share with the court, what name is being used for young Mr. Bailleau?" She said, "Yes, they are calling him Topaz. He ain't no girl, you hear me. He is a man and he needs to act like one, and they ought to be ashamed of themselves. Sitting there like they're so much, like you done so much good with your own child. He ain't so good I tell you. Oh yeah, he say all the right things, cause they sent him to private schools and such. But when is it proper for a man to put his penis into the mouth of a 19 year old girl that happens to be his girlfriend's daughter? This is the family that you want to send my grandbaby with, I won't have it I tell you, I won't. My heart can't stand it your honor. Do you have children?" The judge said, "Yes, I do." My grandmother continued, "How would you feel if someone took advantage of one of your children to pleasure himself when you weren't home, how would that make you feel? I can tell you, It would make you as mad as hell!!!!!" The judge said, "Will that be all Mrs. Bailleau?" She said,

"That will be all fine Sir, and I know you will do the right thing. God Bless you, your honor." She got up and went back to her seat, I was appalled at this level of acting, and again I felt as though I was a part of a Lifetime movie. The judge said, "This is most definitely uncommon but I am going to call Mr. Whalid Bailleau to the stand, please come up Sir." Whalid took the stand without a second thought. The judge asked him, "What do you have to say for yourself young man, I wanted to give you an opportunity to speak on the allegations." Whalid took a deep breath and said, "I thank you your honor for not judging me and giving me a fair chance to tell my side of this. I never maliciously had relations of any type with the daughter of Theresa Bailleau. I was laying asleep on the couch at the home when TriAnn used her door key to let herself in. You see, she doesn't live in the home your honor, only myself, Theresa and Eugene resided there. When I awoke I found TriAnn performing fallatio on me, I immediately push her off me and told her she needed to leave. In the weeks after that she was threatening to tell people that there was more to it if I didn't involve myself with her romantically.

All of this was explained in front of the complete Bailleau family at their Thanksgiving celebration, I don't know why this is coming up again. And also Eugene Bailleau overheard TriAnn in one of her rants when she was attempting to blackmail me and he relayed that information to the family on that day as well. My upbringing has nothing to do with this your honor, my parents did a great job with being there for me and pouring into me and they are doing the same for Eugene, I beg you to see the truth in the testimonies today, because I am sorry but I really feel like I'm at the Academy Awards. I have watched these people with the exception of Mr. Joseph Bailleau, beat, belittle and verbally torture this young man. I do have to say I've never seen Mrs. Bailleau call him out of his name, but she doesn't stop anyone in the family from doing it. And today you could hear in her testimony her true feelings about his sexuality, so I say is that why she allows others to misuse him the way they do. She is the matriarch of this family, if there is anyone that could put a stop to it would'nt it be her, or is it that, the woman of God that we heard speak on family values here today was in

agreement with the treatment? Your honor that is all
I have to say." The judge said, "Thank you, Mr.
Jesper please take your seat."

The judge was in the middle of saying he was
going to have a recess to come up with his decision,
he was interrupted by my Uncle Joe, who said, "Your
honor I'm sorry for being out of order, but I have a
few things to say." The bailiff motioned for my uncle
to sit down. But the judge said, "I'll allow it!" My
uncle was then sworn in and he began, "I've been
sitting here and I'm going to start by saying, I love
my family man, God knows I do but I can't sit by a let
no wrong like this go on. It ain't right. Everything
that the Jespers said today is the truth, and they are
the truth they been takin' damn good care of my nephew
your honor. Whalid was the best thing that ever came
into my sister's house for Lil' Gene. I have been
standin' up for him since he was a lil' dude man, it
was always somethin' bein' said bout my nephew. I'm
talkin' about my sis and her son and daughter callin'
him faggots and stuff from the time he was like 6 or
7. And all this cryin' and stuff, all fake, my sister
and her daughter are more like rival hookers than

mother and daughter, they're fightin' over a young dude right now, that my sis got livin' up in her house. I'm sorry, but you too Mama, it's all fake. And if he wants to be gay, so what and he want to call himself Topaz, so what, it's goin' take some gettin' used to, but hell, I like it. If you got a good bone in your body and a heart in your chest Judge you'll give my nephew to the Jespers to raise him right and love him like I do. I've seen them, I know their heart is real, man. And on a serious note, you will be saving the lives of three or four people, your honor, I've told them if they put their hands on him again, on all I love, I'ma catch a case, it's been too long and I can't take it no more. That's all, man."

There was a one hour recess, the Jespers and I, along with our lawyer went to have lunch and my uncle came too. After his testimony the family wanted nothing to do with him. As we sat and had lunch, I asked my uncle what was he going to do, with him living at my grandmother's house. He said that he had moved out a few weeks after the Thanksgiving situation. He told me again how much he loved me and thanked the Jespers for what they were doing. The

Jespers told him that he was like family as well and he was welcome anytime to come to the house to visit with me. Mr. Foxworth told my uncle that his hat was off to him and that he is a real stand up dude. I didn't say anything, but I was very nervous about the verdict, especially after all that information about Whalid and TriAnn. We finished up, I hardly ate any of my lunch, but we started back to the courtroom, it seemed to be the longest walk I'd ever taken. Once we were back and seated the judge got started, "There was some interesting testimony here today, as well as some disturbing testimony. When a youngster is being treated in a manner not befitting a pet rat it angers me, but when it is being carried out by members of a family it saddens me. Sexuality is never a reason to throw away a child, the statistics on teen suicides and displaced youth are alarming, and a lot of it is due to this kind of ignorance and non-tolerance. If I wasn't wearing a robe and sitting on this bench right now I would say it is due to this kind of foolishness! These are the defining years of his life, and to toy with them in this manner is just unforgivable. What needs to be done is that both families would work

together to get some understanding and get on one
accord to raise this young man up to be not straight,
not bisexual, not Asexual, not homosexual but a
responsible self-motivated citizen. Now if he decides
to be homosexual, which it is apparent that he has and
that's ok, you as a family, all of you, the Bailleaus
and the Jespers should love him unconditionally. But
from what I have seen here today, this kind of bond is
not possible, so that's when it unfortunately comes
across my desk to make decisions for the best interest
of the child. Do you all understand that, I am here
to put the child in the home that I feel will best
prepare him for the life he has ahead! So in saying
that, Mrs. Theresa Bailleau, I have to tell you, it is
a good thing that you work for a utility company,
because you are not a very good actress, before I ever
reviewed the folder filled with statements from
neighbors and other family members and friends of how
you speak to your son, I didn't believe a word you
were saying. Your unease about his sexuality was so
apparent when you stated that you were ok with it, I
knew you were lying. And the same goes for Mrs.
Bailleau, I felt the same unease when you did your

short sermon on the gay life. When you give that

sermon again make sure you back it up with the

corresponding Bible verses. I am seeing the young man

in question and the erratic behavior that you claimed

was being taught to him by the Jespers, they deserve

none of the credit for that, that is all yours. Any

animal continually backed into a corner will

eventually come out fighting, and that is exactly what

happened, you and your daughter backed him into a

corner, and one day the tables turned and

unfortunately it left your daughter with missing

teeth. But again, that is your own fault. Mr. Joseph

Bailleau, I don't know what your relationship will be

with your family from this point, but Sir, know that

you did the right thing. Alright and onto the

Jespers, Mr. and Mrs. Jesper, you have proven to be a

very genuine and loving couple who really have

feelings for this young man. You have done a good job

with your one biological child, he proved that when he

sat here and defended himself against a malicious

claim without yelling and cursing and being taken

outside of his raising. You should be proud, and that

is why I am going to grant you another chance to turn

out another shining citizen to the world. I rule in favor of full legal custody to be given to Wade and Trudy Jesper for Eugene Bailleau on this day of January 9th. I also have a petition here to do a full legal name change, which I also rule in favor of. Young Sir, as of this day you will legally be known as Topaz Jesper." At that point everyone on our side was in tears and shouts of joy. My mom and grandmother were very upset and my mom shouted, "That's a bunch of bullshit! I don't give a fuck, you fuckin' take care of him, you Bitch!" The judge slammed his gavel and said, "One more word Ms. Bailleau and I'll hold you in contempt of court!" He continued, "I am also going to award support payments to the Jespers for the care of Topaz…" he was interrupted by mom's outburst, "What!!!!!" He said, "I'm not going to say it again, one more word and you're going to spend the night in jail! As I was saying, support payments in the amount of $1500.00 monthly will be automatically debited from your paycheck Ms. Bailleau. This will be in effect until Topaz reaches the age of 18 and at that point you will still be responsible for 40% of his college expenses provided he attends college, which I strongly suggest young Mr. Jesper, I see great things in your future son. I just have one word of advice to share with you; look up here at me, and I am saying this to you as a father of five, not a judge. Topaz Jesper, don't ever look back, the future is in front of you, I beg you son, don't you ever look back!"

The tears were steadily rolling down my face as I said to the judge, "I promise I will not." I turned and looked at my new family unit, and my Uncle Joe and said, "God does answer prayers!" Mrs. Jesper said, "Yes he does baby, and this is just the beginning. God loves you and he knows what's best for you."

The End

www.ingramcontent.com/pod-product-compliance
Lightning Source LLC
Chambersburg PA
CBHW080823250626
47160CB00008B/2844